The Big Gamble

By George Harmon Coxe

Originally published in 1956

The Big Gamble

Published by Resurrected Press

This classic book was handcrafted by Resurrected Press. Resurrected Press is dedicated to bringing high quality classic books back to the readers who enjoy them. These are not scanned versions of the originals, but, rather, quality checked and edited books meant to be enjoyed!

Please visit ResurrectedPress.com to view our entire catalogue!

ISBN 13: 978-1-937022-51-8

Printed in the United States of America

FOREWORD

There seems to have always been an affinity between newspapermen and detective fiction. Perhaps this is because the cliché that every reporter has the manuscript for a mystery novel tucked in his desk is, in fact, based on the truth. It may also be, that as the stock in trade of both the detective and the reporter is crime, the crossover is inevitable. There is no question that newspapermen are a stable of the detective novel, either as minor characters, or occasionally, as in *The Big Gamble*, as major ones.

George Harmon Coxe, took those ties to new lengths, with two of his major series characters being newspaper photographers. One, Kent Murdoch, is featured here, while another, Jack "Flashgun" Casey, appeared in numerous stories, novels, radio programs and films. Having worked as a reporter for a number of different papers early in his career, Coxe certainly handles this background honestly and accurately.

Coxe was also one of that group of pulp magazine writers who came out of the 20's and 30's and transformed the detective story into the hard-boiled genre that was to dominate American mystery writing for the next few decades. Coxe, along with the best of this group appeared regularly in *Black Mask* magazine. This group included Dashiell Hammett and Raymond Chandler, as well as authors such as Raoul Whitfield and Jonathan Latimer, who, while less well known today, were avidly read during the period.

Unlike Hammett, Chandler, and Whitfield, Coxe had a long and very successful career. In addition to being a regular at *Black Mask* at its prime, his work appeared in radio serials in the 30's and for several years he wrote for Metro-Goldwyn-Mayer. He continued to be a prolific author of novels, with the last of his 63 books coming out over half a century after his first story.

Resurrected Press is pleased to offer this new edition of one of his classic works, *The Big Gamble*, with hopes that readers new to this master of the hard-boiled genre will appreciate his work.

About the Author

George Harmon Coxe (1901-January 31, 1984) was born in Olean, New York. After a year at Purdue and another at Cornell, he spent a number of years at various papers in California, Florida, and New York. He started writing fiction for pulp magazines in the 20's and became a regular contributor to the premier magazine of the day, *Black Mask*. He wrote over 60 novels, with the last being published in 1975. Several of his series characters, Kent Murdoch and Jack "Flashgun" Casey, were newspaper photographers, and the latter appeared in radio serials and several movies. Coxe also worked for Metro-Goldwyn Mayer for several years. He was president of the Mystery Writers of America and was named by them a Grand Master in 1964.

Greg Fowlkes
Editor-In-Chief
Resurrected Press
www.ResurrectedPress.com

TABLE OF CONTENTS

CHAPTER 1

SATURDAY EVENINGS were usually slow on the Courier. Later, when the midnight closing law of the state shuttered the bars and the frustrated drinkers were turned out on the streets, there would be sporadic fights among the tipsy; still later, a few traffic accidents could be expected, but now, at seven thirty, it was quiet in the studio, a name given to the department that supplied photographers and pictures for the morning, evening, and Sunday editions. Klime was slouched in a chair in the anteroom reading a dog-eared, paper-back novel. Bailey was out cruising in a company radio car, and Kent Murdock, the picture chief, was standing at his desk in the boxlike office that had been constructed by using one corner of the main room and adding two glass-and-wood partitions.

There was a camera on the desk, one of the smaller Graphics, and a soft-leather equipment bag that Murdock had just checked. Not because he had an assignment but because a camera had, by force of habit, become as essential on a weekend trip as a toothbrush. The purpose of this weekend in late September was golf. His clubs, an overnight case, and a small duffel bag were locked in the back of his car, and now he looked up a number in the telephone directory and dialed it.

An immediate busy signal brought forth a whispered: "Nuts." He replaced the phone and continued to himself:

"He probably doesn't want to play anyway, but I said I'd call." He jotted a name and number on a pad, tore off the sheet, and took it out to Klime.

"You on until two?"

"Yeah," said Klime. "Woe is me."

"Do something for me."

Sure.

"I'm going down to the Cape. I've got a golf game in the morning—"

Klime's eyes were still on his book and Murdock reached down and pulled it from his hands.

"I'm listening," Klime said, protesting but not annoyed.

"You've got a golf game."

Murdock gave him the slip of paper. "I saw George Emerly earlier in the week and he said he might go along. I forgot about it until just now and his line's busy and I want to get started."

"So?"

"So call him in an hour or so or whenever you get around to it. Tell him I'll be at the Pine Grove Motel. I'll get a room with twin beds and if he wants to come down tonight he can share it. Anyway, we're teeing off at eight thirty at Catansett if he wants to play."

"Catansett," Klime said. "Eight thirty."

Murdock returned the novel and went back to get his camera and bag. As he closed his office door Klime gave him some advice.

"Golf, hunh?" he said with a grin. "Well, keep your head down, champ."

Once clear of the suburbs, traffic was moderately heavy but it moved swiftly and Murdock made good time in the thickening dusk. He had about twenty or twenty-five minutes of driving left when the state police car slammed past him with the siren moaning, and as he took the next curve he found out why.

Two cars had tangled in the opposite lane, apparently in a rear-end collision. One was off the road on its side, one front wheel still turning; the other had its grill bashed in, the radiator draining on the macadam. By the time Murdock had pulled off the road and stopped, the occupants were standing around feeling their joints and looking for bruises. It was apparent then that no one had been seriously hurt and while the argument began, Murdock reached for his camera.

The gesture was automatic and not predicated on any idea that this was front page material. If he had thought at all it would have occurred to him that from the standpoint of news he might well be wasting film and flashbulbs. But such equipment was cheap and he understood that the time to take pictures was when the opportunity presented itself even if the films were never developed. It was a point he was constantly drumming into his staff and he now practiced what he had preached.

There was a bulb in the fash unit, a filmholder in the slot, one side of which had been exposed. From his bag he took two bulbs and a fresh holder and then he was on the road, taking his first shot from an angle that showed the front of crumpled grill and the cars that had begun to back up behind it. Waiting a moment for the bulb to cool while he pocketed the holder and inserted the fresh one, he ejected it, tossed it up, and caught it a couple of times when he found it still hot, and then threw it into the field at the side of the road. He took his second picture of the upturned car against a background of curious spectators and now, as four or five men got on one side and heaved it upright, he got the last shot just before the two wheels hit the paving.

Back at his car, he moved round the right side and opened the door to deposit the camera on the back seat. As he straightened, some movement caught his eye and he turned to see a squat, black-browed man approaching. He wore slacks and a colorfully patterned sport shirt that hung outside his trousers. Two men, a step or so behind him, stopped when he did.

"You're Murdock, aren't you? From the Courier?"

Murdock nodded, finding the swart face vaguely familiar but unable to place it.

"Terroni," the man said. "Sam Terroni."

"Oh, yes," Murdock said, recalling now that Terroni had spent a couple of years in prison for extortion, the outgrowth of some racket in the trucking business.

"About that picture," Terroni said.

"What picture?"

"The one you took of that car."

By that time Murdock sensed what was coming though he did not know why.

"What makes it important?"

"I'll tell you. I'll level with you. I did some time and I'm out on parole." Terroni rubbed his nose and moved a little closer. "They got a thing called consorting with known criminals...Consorting," he said and spat contemptuously.

"I'm out for a day of blue fishing with some friends." He nodded to the silent pair behind him. "Minding my own business. No trouble, no strain. So we have to run into an accident, and we get out to help, and you come along with that box." He paused again. "My friends happen to have records. Some guy wants to make it real rough for me, that's enough to put me back in the jug for two more years as a parole violator. I don't want that to happen, you know what I mean?"

Murdock nodded and took a breath. He knew what he was going to say. He had said it for years under similar circumstances; so had every other press photographer who had been in business for any length of time. It was standard operating practice and he was patient in his explanation.

"I'm hired to take pictures, Sam. I'm supposed to turn them in. Whether they get printed or not is not up to me."

"Who knows you took it besides you and me? I'm asking a favor, that's all. I don't want trouble—with the law or with you."

Murdock hesitated, but not for long. If the accident had happened in the city on a slow day the chances were the picture would be used. Now, since he had no intention of turning round and driving back with the film, the possibility of it ever being printed was remote. For all of that some basic consideration that could not easily be explained made him shake his head.

"I wouldn't worry about it," he said.

"I am worrying about it."

"I doubt if it ever will be used."

Terroni glanced back at his companions and when he spoke his voice carried a threatening cadence.

"Okay. I've given you a chance to be a good guy. So I better tell you this. If that picture puts me back in the can you can count on two broken arms. I'm not kidding, Murdock."

"Hell," said one of his friends, "what's with all this yackin'. Let's get it now."

The two started to move up and Murdock got his back against the car. For another instant Terroni stood there undecided and then it was too late. What made the difference was the blue-jacketed state policeman who appeared in front of the car and looked sharply at them.

"You'll have to move this car," he said. "If you want more pictures you can pull into that turnoff about a hundred yards ahead and walk back. We've got to get traffic moving."

"Right away," Murdock said.

Terroni was already in retreat before the officer finished. Just before he disappeared behind the car he said:

"You got the message, Murdock?"

"I heard you."

Murdock opened the door, his muscles relaxing, and aware now of a certain sense of relief. He was still not sure why he had been stubborn about releasing the filmholder, but somehow he felt better for not having done so. He shoved over on the seat and turned the ignition key. When the motor caught he reached back to close the door and that was when he saw her standing there looking at him.

"Hello," she said in a voice that was small and rather tentative.

Murdock looked; then blinked again. For she was blonde and young and very pretty as she stood in the opening with the dome light on her face.

"Oh—hello," he said when he found his voice.

"Are you going to Bayview?"

"Yes."

"Could I—could you give me a lift?"

The request was so unexpected that Murdock hesitated.

"Were you in the accident?"

"No. It's just that—well, the boy I was with had some ideas I hadn't expected. He said if I didn't like them I could walk, and I saw you with the camera so—"

She let the sentence dangle, but the red mouth was smiling and there was an appealing sparkle in the blue eyes.

Having just had a brush with trouble from Terroni, Murdock wondered if he was pressing his luck by thwarting a jealous boyfriend, but somehow this did not seem important.

"Get in," he said. "Glad to have you."

She slid in beside him instantly and the dome light went out. He angled onto the road to wait for a signal from the trooper who was directing traffic; then they were rolling and he leaned back and glanced again at the girl. There was enough reflected light from the instrument panel to tell him that she had a cute profile, that the blond hair was cut short and feathered in the back, that the tanned legs were bare beneath the figured cotton dress. She kept her gaze focused straight ahead, and after a bit he introduced himself.

She said, "How do you do," but offered nothing else, so he tried again by asking if she lived in Bayview.

"This summer I have," she said.

"Does your family live here?"

"Oh, no. I work."

"Doing what?"

She hesitated so long he wondered if she had heard him. Then she said: "I'm sort of a nursemaid. I look after some children for a family that have a summer place."

"Then what? Back to school?"

"School?" She laughed shortly. "I finished school. A long time ago."

It came to Murdock then that this girl did not want to talk. Without being actually unfriendly she remained distant and ill at ease. There was an odd stiffness in her body as she sat upright, her back inches from the upholstery, and he got the idea that she was anxious for the ride to be over. And so, reminding himself that she did not have to pay for the lift with conversation, he shrugged and fell silent until the lights of Bayview appeared ahead, a onestreet town that boasted about fifty-five hundred population in the summer and half that in winter. Now, as he eased up on the accelerator, the girl stirred beside him and pointed to the lights of a roadside diner just ahead.

"Would you mind stopping so I could get some cigarettes?"

"I have some," Murdock said.

"I have to get some anyway."

Murdock pulled into the parking space and stopped.

"What kind?"

She told him and fumbled in her purse for some change.

He said he would get them and she said: "Thank you, but I want to pay for them."

She handed him a quarter and a nickel as he got out and he was ready now to accept them without argument.

The truth was he was disappointed. Not that he wanted to pick her up—she seemed a bit young for him— but he had a way of talking with women that usually brought a friendly response. He was casually polite and never familiar unless there was some provocation, and as he stepped inside the diner and glanced about for the cigarette machine he thought: You're losing your charm, kid. You must be getting old.

The idea amused him and he grinned absently when he inserted the coins and pulled the proper plunger. He got the cigarettes and the matches from the tray and turned toward the door, paying no attention to the half dozen customers at the counter. He got the door opened and started down the steps; then he stopped, staring openmouthed at the spot where he had left the car.

For the space was empty, and even though he knew the girl had driven off, he glanced at the other cars parked there to be sure he had made no mistake. Then, cursing softly, he stepped to the ground and moved on out to the highway. A hundred yards away the main street opened up before him and he started walking, a twinge of resentment warping what had heretofore been little more than incredulity.

For the next few minutes he walked with head down, the recently purchased cigarettes still in his fist. He tried to find some answer and the only idea that came to him was that the girl had thought up the cigarette gag to get rid of him, that it had been her intention to steal the car when she had the chance. Had this been the idea from the beginning? Was that business about the fresh boyfriend just part of the act?

And suddenly he stopped speculating and quickened his pace, knowing what he had to do. For while the loss of the car bothered him, the camera and his equipment on the back seat worried him even more.

Worry built inside him as he strode along the sidewalk dodging the Saturday night shoppers and their children. Three blocks ahead was the police station and the chief was a long-time acquaintance of his. It was going to be a bit embarrassing when he related his story, but there was no alternative now. This was what he told himself, but even so his eyes were busy as he took note of each parked car he passed. When he came to the parking lot that adjoined the railroad station, he stopped to get a good look, moving in from the sidewalk and seeing the gleam of the tracks that paralleled the main street for some distance.

A moment later he saw a car that looked familiar silhouetted against the brick wall of the station and he angled that way, hurrying now, the certainty growing in him that this was it. A glimpse of the license plate told him he was right. The lights had been turned off and the seat was empty. When he opened the door he saw the key in the switch, and a second glance told him his camera and equipment bag were still on the back seat.

"Well, I'll be damned," he said, and climbed in.

CHAPTER 2

WHEN KENT MURDOCK drove out on the street and turned toward the motel he had discarded his original theory that the blonde had planned to steal his car. The alternative that now came to him suggested the ride was legitimate and that the cigarette gambit was nothing more than a way to get rid of him once her objective had been reached. The conclusion, that she must have been a little afraid of him, was not flattering, but having accepted it, he tried to dismiss the incident, and the girl.

It was about three miles to the Pine Grove Motel, and as he made the turn into the driveway his headlights focused briefly on a car that was just coming out. It was a small gray convertible, and with the window down, he caught a glimpse of the driver. The face seemed familiar, and by the time he had stopped opposite the office he knew this was Paul Herrick, a musician who led the orchestra at a night club a mile or so on the other side of Bayview.

The sign in the drive said:

THE PINE GROVE
FREE RADIO
NO VACANCY

The main building was a white Cape Cod cottage containing the office, a lounge, and a lunch room, with the owner's quarters above. Behind it on the fringe of a small pine grove stood eight smaller cottages, each containing two units. The No Vacancy sign did not bother Murdock because he had telephoned ahead, and now he walked into the lobby, aware that the lounge was in semi-darkness and that the television was blasting out some lines that could only have been written for a western. The man who sat in the small chair by the doorway watching the show stood up when he saw Murdock and came round the desk.

The clock on the wall behind it said: 9:28.

"Evening, Mr. Murdock."

"Hi, Charlie. You got my reservation, didn't you?"

"Oh, sure. Number fifteen, like you asked for."

Murdock registered, put down the number of his license plates, and counted out ten dollars.

"There's an outside chance a Mr. Emerly may be in," he said. "If he comes put him in with me...Now what about tomorrow? You want to go out?"

Charlie Lane considered the request, a stocky man with a round, deeply tanned face that was crisscrossed with wrinkles which came not from worry but from an almost constant exposure to the sun and weather. He was fortyseven years old, a widower for as long as Murdock had known him. His only vice, except for an occasional bout with the bottle, was gambling, particularly the horses.

What was more important to Murdock was that Charlie was what might be called a professional caddy and in this profession he was tops.

"You got a game?" he asked finally.

"With Doctor Markey. At Catansett. Eight thirty. If I'm going to take him tomorrow I have to have you."

Charlie Lane grinned. "You wouldn't need me if you concentrated... Why, sure," he said. "Be glad to go, Mr. Murdock."

"I'll pick you up here at eight fifteen... Oh, by the way, do you know Paul Herrick?"

"Over at the Blue Heron? Sure."

"Didn't he just leave here?"

"I didn't see him."

"I thought I saw him driving out."

"Could be, Mr. Murdock, but if he was here he didn't stop in the office."

Murdock nodded, took his key, and went out to his car. When he pulled into the carport on the left side of the last cottage he noticed the light in the other unit, and as he cut his motor he could hear the radio playing, though there was no car in the end port.

Unlocking the rear deck, he took out his case and duffel bag. He got the camera bag over his shoulder, the camera in his free hand. He had a little trouble unlocking the door, but when he got the light on he staggered over to the bureau and unloaded. He opened the case to take out his toilet kit, the clean linen, the pajamas and robe. He left the golf shoes, sox, and sweater in the duffel bag but took out a polo shirt and put it in a drawer. Remembering the plateholder in his pocket, he tossed it into the duffel bag and slid out of his jacket.

He had started for the bathroom to wash and comb his hair when his glance skimmed the camera. Suddenly he stopped. Turning from the hips, he looked back at the camera, focusing now as he completed the turn. Only then did he realize that there must be still a third theory about that blonde.

For the filmholder that had been left in the camera, the one he had used for the last two accident pictures, was gone.

Certain of this, but not yet understanding why, he stood quite still, dark eyes somber beneath the straight black brows, not looking at the camera now, not looking at anything in the room. He slid his palm absently over straight dark hair that was threaded with gray at the temples, and his angular, well-boned face was impassive but not grim.

A muscle twitched in the hinge of his jaw as he made up his mind and then, not hurrying, he put on his jacket and switched off the light.

About two thirds of the distance along Bayview's main street and standing next to a service station was a tiny concrete cube with a neon sign on the roof that said: Taxi. Two cabs were parked near the door when Murdock stepped into the office and spoke to the dispatcher, a bluejawed husky in a khaki shirt.

"A blonde doll?" the man said as his glance slid to a skinny youth who had tipped his chair back against the wall. "On Main Street about twenty minutes ago? Was that you, Eddie?"

"Could be," Eddie said. "Who wants to know?"

"I'm from the Boston Courier." Murdock showed his press card while he improvised. "She stepped off the sidewalk into my car. By the time I could find a place to stop I'd lost her. I don't think she's hurt but I don't want to get sued either. I'd like to talk to her, but I thought I'd ask you before I went down and spoke to Chief Nickerson."

The dispatcher thought it over, shrugged faintly, and glanced at Eddie. "So tell the man," he said. "It's no skin off your nose."

"She went to the Blue Heron."

"Did she go into the club?"

"Around back," Eddie said. "There's a couple of cottages for some of the help. The flat-roofed one, last door."

The Blue Heron stood on a slight rise, and on a clear day there was a view of the Bay. A low, gray-shingled building, it had blue shutters on the windows, a small marquee, and a uniformed boy to park cars for those who wanted such service. Murdock had been there several times but never during the day and now, not sure whether he could drive behind the building, he eased his car round the edge of the parking space until he saw a sand-andgravel road angling to the left.

Smoke from charcoal-broiled steaks tickled his nostrils as he idled past the kitchen and service entrance and then he saw the cottage another fifty feet beyond. Grayshingled like the main building, it stood opposite a flatroofed structure built like a miniature motel. Two cars were parked to one side of the cottage and Murdock stopped beyond the flat-roofed building, turned, and drove back to the first door.

The blonde was very surprised to see him. She was wearing a long cotton robe, one hand holding the front edges to keep it closed snugly about her. She stepped back in her surprise, her lids blinking before the scowl came, and by that time Murdock was inside a longish room that had twin beds, twin chests, a vanity painted in blue, some wicker chairs, and a worn, fibre rug. One open door disclosed a lighted bath, another hinted at what might have been a small kitchen.

"Oh—you."

That was all she could manage in the first few seconds.

"Yeah," Murdock said casually. "Me."

She had backed to the center of the room and now she faced him resolutely, no longer looking so young but still pretty, a tightness in the red mouth and her gaze hostile after that first moment of uncertainty.

"All right," she said, not loud but harshly. "What do you want?"

"I don't know," Murdock said. "Maybe an apology."

"For what?"

"For stealing my car."

"Okay. I apologize. I was in a hurry... Now get out."

"Sure. Just as soon as you give me back that filmholder you lifted."

"What filmholder?"

Murdock hesitated and his right brow climbed a quarter of an inch, an unconscious gesture that at times gave him a look that could be sardonic, quizzical, doubtful, or suspicious, depending on what was happening to the dark eyes. Now, more puzzled than annoyed by her attitude, he found her defiance formidable and wondered if it could be founded on fear.

"Do you know Sam Terroni?"

"Sam who?"

He repeated the last name and she shook her head.

"Never heard of him."

He tried again, a note of impatience in his voice as his irritation mounted.

"It wasn't your idea, was it? So who did you steal it for?"

"I don't know what you're talking about."

Murdock glanced about the room. When he realized his chances of searching it were not very good he decided to see if a bluff might help.

"All right," he said. "If you won't play ball with me let's go see the police. Get some clothes on and—"

"Police?"

Her voice rose and for an instant the blue eyes looked doubtful; then she reacted in a way that was as daring as it was unexpected. Releasing the front of her robe she let it hang free, exposing a body that might have measured 37-24-35 and was seductively molded. The legs, thighs, and shoulders were tanned like her face. The area between the brief panties and the brassiere was also tanned but of a lighter shade. Then, as Murdock stared, she put her fingers into the top of the brassiere and tightened her fist.

"Police," she said furiously. "If you don't get out of here and let me alone I'm going to rip this thing and scream my head off. Maybe you can think of a story the cops will believe but I doubt it... Now get out!"

For a brief second Murdock nearly called her. He was going to say, "Go ahead and rip it and I'll buy you a new one." That was what he had in mind, but something in her eyes stopped him cold. Suddenly he knew she meant it and just as suddenly he was scared.

He could feel the sweat pores open as his imagination pictured his predicament when the help came running in.

He could see himself squirming and protesting. He could almost feel the bruises and lacerations that might follow. He had thrown the bluff and she had called it, and he said, hastily:

"All right, all right. Take it easy."

Then, before he could prove he meant it, the door banged open and two men walked in.

"Was that you yelling, Lucille?" the big one said.

"This guy bothering you?" said the other.

The girl looked right at Murdock, her head tossing defiantly as she snatched the robe about her torso.

"Yes."

They were moving toward Murdock then, both very neat in their dinner jackets, one about his size and build —moderately tall and perhaps one hundred and seventyfive pounds—the other three inches taller and forty pounds heavier.

"You want we should toss him out, Lucille?" the big one said.

"Yes."

"Okay, chum," they said and now they were on either side of Murdock, a hand on each arm.

Murdock swallowed and kept his muscles loose. The odds were prohibitive now and he understood that resistance would probably mean a full quota of lumps. Momentarily accepting defeat in his battle with the blonde, he decided to go quietly and hope for the best.

They walked past the girl, Murdock in the middle, until they reached the open door. Here they hesitated while the big man said: "Did you say toss, Lucille?"

"Yes," said the girl in the same flat tone.

Apparently all this was meant literally because that is what happened. Before Murdock realized it the hands tightened on his arms. Two more hands clamped on the backs of his knees as the pair stooped slightly. When they straightened Murdock came off the floor in a sitting position, there was a small backward swing, and then he was going forward, feet first and arms waving as they let go and he sailed through the doorway.

He was too busy trying to keep from crashing on the back of his neck to have any immediate feeling of chagrin or humiliation, and when he landed he hit solidly on his buttocks and skidded three feet, on the grass fortunately, otherwise he surely would have lost the seat of his trousers. As he turned his head and got his breath back he saw that the two men had followed him out and stood looking down, hands on hips as they waited for his next move.

"That was nice, Felix," the slender man said.

"Neat," said the big man. "You okay, Mac?" he said to Murdock.

To his great surprise there was very little anger in Murdock. There was nothing vicious about his ejection and there was imagination in the method. The situation was so ludicrous, so unexpected, and so quickly done that he took a moment to sit there and understand that in a way he had deserved what he got. He had tried to scare a girl who was more resourceful than he had bargained for, and while he had no intention of quitting so easily he chuckled softly as he rose and brushed himself off.

"No."

"Good."

"That your car?" said Felix.

"Use it," said his companion.

"And don't come back."

Murdock opened the door and glanced round.

"Okay to go in and get a drink?"

"Sure," said Felix. "In there—"

"—you're a customer," said the other.

"Out back here—"

"You're off limits."

They were still standing there watching him as he climbed in and started the motor. As he drove off he saw in the rearview mirror that they were following him.

CHAPTER 3

THE BLUE HERON was doing a big business on this Saturday night. Although Murdock did not know it when he went in, he learned that this was the last night before the place closed for the season, and now the bar was filled with those who eschewed the minimum charge, most of the tables were taken, and the floor was crowded with couples dancing to Paul Herrick's music.

There was a small table over in one corner, not a choice location but one that was situated so one could see the bar, the main entrance, and the doorway leading to the service quarters. It was also fairly close to the piano, and when Murdock had claimed it from the waiter he went into the men's room to wash his hands and comb his hair. There were no grass stains that he could see on his gray flannel slacks, and his Shetland jacket was neat enough, so he went back to his table and ordered a drink.

Herrick's band—piano, bass, drums, guitar, trumpet, and clarinet—was playing a current Hit-Parade favorite based on three chords and featuring a repetitive melody that was as monotonous as it was banal. Murdock stood it as long as he could and then stepped up behind Herrick, who grinned in recognition and then nodded as Murdock said:

"How about making like Fats Waller for one chorus of something?"

"Right."

"Stop at the table when you finish the set if you can." Back at his table he sipped his drink and listened, and presently the chorus ended and Herrick transposed into "Ain't Misbehavin'," picking up the beat a bit as he took the solo. With his eyes closed Murdock thought he was listening to Waller. That was one reason he liked Herrick.

He had studied, he knew music, and he had a big left hand that worked on chords and tenths just as hard as his right, not an easy thing to find these days when most piano players did acrobatics on the treble and threw in an occasional bass chord just to prove they had two hands. Now, as Herrick finished the chorus, he glanced over his shoulder and grinned; then the band picked up the last chorus and hit it as if they enjoyed it. The resulting applause said someone beside Murdock approved, and when the band struck up another tune of the day, he shut out the sound and began to think.

For there was a stubborn streak in Murdock and his futile session with the blonde Lucille and the two bouncers served only to increase his desire to find out why she had stolen the filmholder, and who wanted it. Sam Terroni was the logical suspect. But what had the girl been doing out on the highway in the first place? How did she happen to be there and who thought up the gimmick about the fresh boyfriend?

The question made him glance round and he saw Felix and his pal at one end of the bar counting the house and looking for trouble. And now, frustrated by his lack of answers but holding no grudge, Murdock signaled the waiter and asked who the fellow was with Felix.

"Nate Tishman."

"Ask him and Felix to have a drink," Murdock said, "and put it on my check."

He watched the waiter scurry away, and as his gaze shifted he spotted Lucille moving around the perimeter of the room. A moment later her occupation and connection with the Blue Heron became at once apparent. The tanned shapely legs were encased in sheer nylon stockings now and she wore a flaring knee-length skirt and a tight bodice. Around the neck and across the bare shoulders was a strap, at the end of which hung a tray of cigarettes. Her eyes were busy as she wandered among the tables and when she made a sale her face would light up in an attractive smile, but she did not see Murdock until he called.

"Oh, miss."

She turned, stared, and stopped still, the tentative smile fading. She waited there as though making up her mind; finally she came over to him.

"Do you want something?" she asked stonily.

"I'll take that filmholder if you have it handy."

"Sorry," she said, very cool now. "I'm only selling cigarettes tonight."

"How about some Chesterfields, regular." He watched her consult her wares, select a pack, and tear off one corner.

"I'm a customer now, you know," he said. "You should treat me with respect."

She did not look at him as she put the cigarettes and matches on a tray and placed it before him, but he thought he caught a glimmer of a smile as she said:

"I always treat the customer with respect. Even when he's stubborn. It works both ways, you know."

Murdock found a half dollar and put it on the tray. She picked it up and tipped it so the coin slid into her hand.

"Thank you, sir," she said, making it sound demure, like the girl who had wanted a ride.

As she stepped back the waiter touched Murdock's arm and pointed toward the bar. The two bouncers were grinning at him and holding their glasses up to acknowledge the drinks he had bought them. He returned the gesture with a salute of his own, aware now that Lucille had witnessed the by-play. She gave him a glance that was both curious and puzzled, as though she realized what he had done and could not understand it.

"You're not sore, are you?" she said.

"No. There may be some stiffness in a certain area of my anatomy in the morning, but I'm not sore. Just curious," Murdock said. "I'm going to keep on being curious."

He ordered another drink as the girl went away, and as he watched her a brief burst of light tinted the room. He knew what it was without looking, but he turned to locate the source. The small, neatly made brunette with the camera was just turning away from a foursome at a table near the dance floor and, like that, the idea came to him. This was not the city where a central processing room could service three or four nightclubs. If there was a house photographer there had to be a developing room in the club, and he knew now that he was going to have a look at it before he left. So long as there was a chance that the blonde had brought the filmholder here—

The thought hung there as the chair opposite him was pulled out, and then he gave his attention to the man who had eased onto it. Until then he had not been aware that the music had stopped; now he took Paul Herrick's offered hand and asked him what he'd have. The waiter, just bringing Murdock's bourbon and water, went back to get a Scotch-on-the-rocks and Herrick said:

"Haven't seen you in quite a while."

"I have a golf game in the morning so I thought I'd stop and give you a listen. That Waller chorus was nice. Now if you could give me one by Tatum."

"Hah!" said Herrick and grinned. "Who can? Who could? I could give you maybe eight bars before my hands got cramped." He shook his head, his face sobering. "And don't think anybody's going to take his place."

He leaned back to let the waiter put his drink down and then stared at the glass, a tall, rangy man of thirty or so with light-brown hair worn short but not in a crew cut, and an easy smile that showed nice teeth; a good-looking man by any standard, a handsome one by most.

"You've got the hands for it," Murdock said.

"Yeah. And some of the technique. But a lot of what Art had came from somewhere inside his head, and even if you had that it wouldn't sound quite the same. He put a lot of weight on a keyboard; it came out big... They don't play like that any more. They don't even try. The young guys today are all trying to imitate Shearing or Peterson and that's not easy either. Wilson, Chittison, Guarnieri, Larkin, when he wants to—they play so you can hear the left hand but there aren't many . . . Well, cheers."

They drank. Over at the piano the guitar player started noodling. He finally found a chorus of something he liked and Murdock said:

"Not too bad."

"Better than some who carry a card for that instrument."

Murdock was still keeping score on the photographer. She now had three orders and he watched where she went. In another fifteen or twenty minutes she'd be out to show her wares and that would be the time to have a look.

"I heard this is your last night," he said. "What then?"

"I've got a four-week spot in the city," Herrick said. "The Melody Grill starting a week from Monday. I'm only taking the bass, guitar, and drums. After that"—the big grin came again—"I'm getting married."

"I heard something about that. Congratulations."

"Thanks. And they're in order. She's a wonderful girl. Not only that, her old man's a V.P. in a New York ad agency that does a lot of TV. He likes the way I play and he's listened to some arrangements. He says maybe I can do some arranging for some of the agency shows. I hope so. I'm tired of playing in traps."

Murdock said it sounded good and then digressed.

"Who's the cigarette girl?"

"Lucille Dunn. Kind of cute, hunh?"

"Very."

"She's a nice kid. The only thing is she pesters the hell out of me."

"Oh?"

"Wants to be a singer."

"Can she?"

"A little. She phrases pretty well and she has some ideas but her voice is about this big." He held his thumb and forefinger an eighth of an inch apart.

"How big is Julie London's voice?"

Herrick glanced up and chuckled. "You've got a point. Also some of the numbers Peggy Lee does. That's what Lucille's been selling me and she could be right."

He finished his drink. "But she needs the kind of engineers they have in studios, experts who can take that little voice and twist the right dials and make something good come out. With the P.A. system they have here, and in most places like it, it don't sound quite right. I finally did a couple of arrangements for her in the right key. One thing, she's no quitter. She might make it yet... Well, I've got to hit another table before I go back on the stand. Some fans down from the city. Thanks for the drink."

Murdock was ready when the photograph-girl came out through the green curtains behind the bandstand. A glance at the bar told him the bouncers' attention was momentarily occupied with other matters, so he stood and circled toward the doorway. The short corridor beyond was deserted. There was a door on each side and one at the end and he tried the first one on the right. The smell told him this was the place and he groped for a switch that snapped on a tinted, low-watt bulb in the ceiling.

It was a very small workroom indeed but sufficient for its purpose with a sink, some trays, a counter, a paper rack; an inexpensive enlarger and easel, a small ferrotyper. A wire strung from wall to wall had seven or eight negatives clipped to it, but a glance was enough to tell Murdock that these were all taken in the club. He had stepped back, ready now to admit defeat, when he spotted the large wastebasket beneath the counter. On impulse, he pulled it out and bent down to inspect the spoiled prints that had been discarded here.

He realized then that some had been torn into small pieces and he began to gather them, spreading them face up on the counter, aware too that small strips of cut negative were mixed with the prints.

The conclusion that came immediately to mind proved to be the right one. He had enough fragments of torn prints to be positive they came from the films he had exposed at the scene of the accident, and one strip of negative, cleancut, apparently by shears or the paper cutter, was sufficient to tell him that both prints and negatives had been destroyed.

He straightened then, sweeping the fragments back into the basket. He kicked it under the counter, his gaze darkly brooding as his mind again grappled with the puzzle. What stopped him was the rattle of the doorknob. It sounded loud in the stillness, startling him so that there was only time to turn from the counter. Then he was face to face with the little brunette and her camera. She stopped instantly, a frightened gasp rising in her throat as her eyes stretched wide. They slid beyond him and came back. He could see her swallow and wet her lips, and now the reaction came and her voice was both indignant and resentful.

"What are you doing here?"

Murdock gave her a big smile. He made his voice hearty.

"Just looking around. I'm a photographer from the Courier. I just wanted to see how you operated down here in the sticks."

"Oh," she said, her eyes still not believing him.

"Don't give you much room, do they?" He eased past her and gained the opening. "Tell you what," he said. "If things are slow I'll give you an order. That is, if you can get that cigarette girl to sit down at my table and get in the picture."

"Well—" She watched him back into the hall and her voice was still doubtful. "I don't know. I'll ask her."

"You do that," Murdock said, still hearty. "Sorry I startled you."

He moved quickly then, grateful that he'd been able to talk himself out of a situation that might have brought Felix and Nate on his neck. One bouncing was enough for one night, and as he came through the curtains he gave the room a quick inspection to make sure he had not been noticed.

At his table he drained his glass thirstily and decided he could use one more. He got the waiter's eye, ordered a refill and told him to bring the check. Then, his mind going once again to the puzzle, he saw that certain assumptions could be made. He ticked them off as he tested them.

A. Lucille Dunn had stolen the filmholder.

B. She had brought it here.

C. Either personally or by telephone she had been ordered to have the films developed to make sure she had the right ones.

D. A more tenuous assumption was that someone connected with the Blue Heron had planned the operation. All this brought him again to the question of Who, and as his thoughts turned back he found himself considering a man named Carl Darrow, who, in addition to certain real-estate holdings in Boston and Miami, also owned, if rumor was to be credited, a substantial piece of this club.

Just why Darrow should be interested in that accident was beyond Murdock's powers of comprehension at the moment, but as his drink came and he paid his check he glanced again at the bar and realized once more that coincidence had to be accepted as part of life's pattern.

For Carl Darrow now stood in the alleyway between the bar and the tables talking to Paul Herrick. The guitar player had taken over the piano. The two bouncers were still waiting for trouble and the clock over the bar said it was eleven thirty-five.

Whatever the discussion was about it claimed both men's attention. They glanced at the bandstand from time to time and gestures augmented their words until Herrick stepped back, spread both hands palms upward, and turned away. Darrow watched him disappear through the doorway to the service quarters and then walked slowly over to Felix and Nate. They huddled briefly and it seemed to Murdock that at one point all three turned to glance at his table. This, he knew, could have been nothing more than his imagination, and presently he lost interest in the mental game he had been playing. He finished his drink, glanced again at his watch, and saw that if he hurried he could be in bed by midnight. . . .

The night was cool and clear as he drove back through Bayview and along the highway to the motel. The baby moon that had been high earlier was well down at this hour, and as he wheeled into the drive and came up the slight grade the only illumination other than the floodlighted sign came from a dim glow in the office, and from the windows of the unit adjoining his own.

There was still no car in the last port but he could hear a radio playing faintly as he cut his motor and locked the doors. The sound was much more distinct once he was in his room. He could easily follow the tune the disk jockey had selected, and because the night was otherwise so still it seemed to him that the music grew louder the longer he listened.

He grumbled about this as he slipped off his jacket and hung it up. He opened up one of the beds and sat down to take off his shoes and then he stopped to glare at the wall beyond from which the music sounded.

"Damn it," he said, half aloud, "why do they have to have free radio here? Why can't they use those quarter machines like they have on radios in most motels?"

The chances were that the next-door tenant had gone off and forgotten the radio, and there was no telling how long he would be gone. What made it bad now was the fact that the three drinks had done nothing to make Murdock sleepy; they had, if anything, stimulated even more the mental gymnastics he had been occupied with ever since he had missed his car. He could not get to sleep with that music on—he listened as the music stopped and the commercial started—and he knew it. Then he thought of Charlie Lane, who had a small room adjoining the office, part of his payment for keeping an eye on things from six o'clock until midnight.

"Charlie'll have a master key," he said. "Charlie can turn the damn thing off."

He donned his jacket again and stepped outside, leaving his door ajar. Maybe, he thought, I ought to knock first. If anyone is in I can ask him to cut down on the volume. The knock went unanswered and as he stepped back he moved close to the window. The blinds were angled downward so that from where he stood he could see only the foot of one bed and a section of a scatter rug. Wishing he were a few inches taller, he went to the next window and tried again. This gave him a glimpse of the area between the beds. Here there was something on the floor, but he could not identify it. It was something bulky and white, like a bundle wrapped in cloth, and when he realized he was only wasting time with such tactics he wheeled and marched toward the office, still grumbling.

He knew where Charlie's room was, so he rounded the corner of the main building and scratched on the screen as he called out. After an interval of several seconds he got a reply.

"Yeah?" a sleepy voice said. "Who is it?"

"Me. Murdock... Look, Charlie, some stupe in the room next to mine went off and left the radio on. You've got a key, haven't you? Can't you come over and turn it off? I can't play golf in the morning with that thing on all night."

"Okay, Mr. Murdock," Charlie said. "Wait 'till I get my slippers and a robe."

Murdock was waiting when Charlie Lane came out, his hair tousled and a cigarette in his mouth. When he got a light he said:

"It happens once in a while. We've had other complaints."

They walked in silence then and when they reached the proper door Charlie knocked twice before using his key. He moved into the lighted room and Murdock followed because he was curious about the object he had seen on the floor. He was aware, even then, that neither bed had been used. A print dress had been spread out on one of them and beside it was a pair of clean stockings. He noticed that much before Charlie stopped abruptly and stiffened in front of him and now, wondering why, Murdock's gaze darted beyond and he found the answer as Charlie spoke.

"Good God!"

Murdock saw the legs first, bare to the lower thighs. He had to move up to see more; he had to push past Charlie, who was rooted to the spot, eyes wide open and jaw slack. He saw then that the woman lay face down, her head near the night table and the long blond hair spread out fanlike to obscure the side of her face. She was clad in an opaque white slip, the straps on her shoulders paralleling those on her brassiere. One stocking lay in a small heap next to a pair of high-heeled spectator pumps; the other was around her neck.

Not yet knowing the answer, Murdock went to one knee beside the torso, seeing now the red-leather pocketbook that had been tipped over on its side, the jaws gaping. He put his hand on her arm and then jerked it back because the flesh seemed cold to his touch. Slowly then the horror grew in him and he crouched there, muscles tensing as the shock made itself felt. Finally, somewhere behind him, Charlie Lane found his voice.

"What's the matter with her?" he whispered hoarsely. "She—she ain't dead, is she, Mr. Murdock? . . . She ain't dead?"

Murdock looked again at the arms and hands, which were resting on the rug, head high, the fingers curled slightly inward. The nails were red but there were no rings, and finally he again took one wrist in his hand, finding it somewhat stiff and certain now of the definite coolness of the skin. He drew a slow breath and exhaled noisily as he tried to get his thoughts in hand. He rocked back on one foot.

"I'm afraid so, Charlie," he said wearily. "Do you know who she is?"

"No. I see her come in but I didn't watch her register."

"Alone?"

"N—o. Seems like there was a man in the car."

"But she registered?"

"That's right."

"Would you know the man if you saw him again?"

"No. Never did get a look at his face. Anyway it was getting kind of dark then."

Murdock leaned over the body to pick up the pocketbook. It was a long reach, and when he got it by his fingertips and started to lift, it slipped from his grasp and fell upside down, the contents emptying on the rug. He finally rose and stepped nearer the other bed and began to replace the compact and lipstick, the silver cigarette case, the lighter, tissues, gum, bobby pins. That left the pinseal leather wallet which was what he had been after in the first place.

It was the sort that folds lengthwise to be held in place by a strap and button, and when he snapped this open, he saw the attached change purse, the bill compartment holding three or four twenty-dollar notes, and the identification he sought. He read the words aloud, his voice hollow as the wonderment grew in him. For he suddenly understood that he knew this woman, would have recognized her instantly had the blond hair not obscured her features.

"Mrs. Hazel Franklin," he said. "Hazel Franklin?"

He bent quickly now to brush the hair aside, to know that the identification was right, to see the cyanosis that had set in to color the face, to note the marks on the throat the stocking had made.

When he rose again the stiffness had gone from his body. He looked at Charlie and the man looked back, his mouth still gaping before he swallowed.

"You know her, Mr. Murdock?"

"Yeah. I know her. Somebody strangled her."

"Jesus!" said Charlie and swallowed again.

CHAPTER 4

HIS JOB as picture chief had kept Kent Murdock much too close to a desk for his own liking. The money was good —better than he could have made pushing a button on a camera—and the hours were regular. But when something happened, something that called for action and ingenuity and a maximum of speed, he could seldom take part except vicariously. Perhaps it was some resentment of such restrictions that now made him react like the press photographer he had once been.

Standing here alone with Charlie Lane in the presence of murder, knowing that the police must be summoned but knowing too that he had an exclusive for the Courier, he glanced at his watch and began to think in terms of editions, press runs, and time limits. It was a minute or so after midnight. He could make the Courier by one thirty.

By phoning ahead and telling the city room he was bringing pictures there would be time to get a bulletin in the city edition; if they wanted to re-plate for a picture it could be carried in most of that run and all of the final. This was the sort of enterprise the Courier paid its photographers for, and at the moment Murdock was again one of the staff. If there was a little trouble later with the authorities it was nothing he couldn't handle. The important thing was time, and now he spoke to Charlie as he turned away and started for his room.

"Hold everything, Charlie," he said. "I'll be right back."

It took him less than a minute to get the camera, an extra bulb, and a fresh filmholder. He checked the aperture and shutter speed and focused from a spot near the foot of the bed. When he had his shot he ejected the hot bulb on the bed and reversed the holder. He stood up on the bed to get a better angle, and the other bed was in the way so he asked Charlie to push it back a foot or so. As the bulb went off he knew this was the better shot. The torso, head, and hands were in the proper perspective now. He was also aware of a bright metallic object that lay close to one leg of the night table. He had not noticed it before because it was in the shadow, but the burst of light picked it out. Charlie noticed it too and bent to retrieve it.

"This yours, Mr. Murdock? It's a tie-clasp."

Murdock glanced down at his rumpled tie and saw that the clip he had been wearing was gone. He said: "Yes," and when Charlie tossed it to him he clipped it in place automatically.

"Come on," he said, taking the man's arm and leading him toward the door. "Leave this place alone."

"But—what about the police?"

"We'll get them. You can call."

"Me?"

"I'm going back to the paper."

"Now?"

They were in Murdock's room by this time and when he had pocketed the filmholder, he snapped off the light and made sure the door was locked. Remembering the public telephone booth near the office, he mentioned it. "While I'm talking to the paper you go in and get some clothes on. As soon as I take off you can telephone the Bayview police."

"Yeah, but—what do I tell em?"

"Tell them the truth. Tell them just what we did and say I had to get these pictures to town. Tell them I'll be back just as soon as I can. Have you got it?"

Charlie was still unconvinced, but he agreed. He sighed heavily and scratched his head.

"All right," he said. "If you say so."

There was very little traffic on the road at that hour and Murdock held an even sixty except when he approached the center of some town or village. The outskirts of the city were almost as deserted, and when he stopped in the parking lot adjacent to the Courier building it was just one twenty-five.

Klime, still on duty, was nodding in his chair and Murdock shook him awake and gave him the filmholder.

"All right, all right," Klime said as he started for the corridor which gave on the developing cubicles. "Some golf game you had."

Murdock dropped into a chair and called upstairs to bring the night city editor up to date. When he finished he said:

"Do you want to put somebody on the story? I've got to get back there and if you've got a man he can ride with me.

The city editor thought it over. "We might, at that. I haven't got anybody here. I might wake up young Berry. He's an eager beaver. When're you leaving?"

"I can wait a half hour or so."

"Okay. Let me check."

Murdock hung up and got a cigarette out. He had been moving under pressure for quite a while and it felt good to relax. It felt good for about three minutes, until his mind began to work again and he realized that there was one thing more that would help the story. The picture of the dead woman was all right, but it would be better if he had a photograph of the woman alive so that the readers could know what she looked like. In some ways such a picture might be even more important than the more dramatic one he had brought with him. The trouble was there would be nothing in the morgue upstairs about Hazel Franklin and—

His thoughts hung there a moment and then began to build. He remembered the address in the woman's wallet.

It was no more than a five-minute drive from here and he had a little gizmo in his own wallet, given him a long time ago by a private detective named Jack Fenner, that would probably open the door of the dead woman's apartment. A slow grin began to work on his mouth and crinkle the corners of his eyes as he ground out his cigarette and the idea took shape. Later the local police would be going over that apartment, once they had been notified by Bayview, but for a while at least there was an opportunity for him if he wanted it.

"What the hell," he said softly, and stood up. "Why not?"

Four doors opened from the quiet third-floor hall of Hazel Franklin's apartment building and the one Murdock sought was on the right, rear. The device Fenner had given him was already in his hand, a thin, blue-steel blade rounded at one end and perhaps a half inch wide. When he had tried the knob and found the door locked, he inserted the light but flexible blade between the molding and the casing so that it engaged the sloping surface of the bolt. When he felt it start to slide he applied more pressure and suddenly there was a faint click and the door was open.

He took time to replace the blade and then he stepped inside, groping along the right-hand wall until he found the electric switch which activated the two lamps on the end tables flanking the davenport. In that first instant as he closed the door behind him he was surprised by the elegance of the room, but before he could speculate about it he saw the open drawers of the kneehole desk that stood between two windows, and the papers that had been scattered about.

The answer came at once, bringing with it an odd tension, and he stood listening, letting his glance touch the wall-to-wall carpeting, the upholstered pieces, the floor lamps, and moving then to what might have been intended for a dining alcove but now had the look of an improvised workroom with its table desk, typewriter and stand, a bookcase, another stand with a one-drawer filing cabinet. Someone had been here before him.

Someone had been searching this room. He could not be sure if the intruder had found what he was looking for,

but when he understood how that person had gained
entrance to the place he was forced to accept the
probability that the searcher was also the killer.

For he remembered the pocketbook he had examined
when he had looked for some identification. He tried to
catalogue again the contents, and one thing was missing.
Keys. A woman would have keys in her bag; at least one
key. There would have to be a key to this apartment. And
there had been no such key.

The tension was working now, quietly but
nonetheless real, as he moved over to the desk and sat
down in the chair. The papers in the drawers were
disordered and a Manila folder had been jammed among
them. Those that had been spilled on the floor seemed to
be mostly letters and receipts, and as he bent over, the
name on one which lay face up caught his eye. When he
picked it up he saw it was an agreement which had been
signed by Hazel Franklin and George Emerly. In essence
the agreement said that the woman was to get twenty-
five per cent of all money received by Emerly based on
ideas originally conceived by Hazel's late husband Ted
Franklin.

The terms of the agreement and the reason for it
meant nothing to Murdock; the names did. For George
Emerly was the one-time newspaperman turned free-
lance writer, whom Murdock had tried to work into his
Sunday golf game, and Ted Franklin, who had been killed
in Hungary while representing a news magazine, had
once worked for the Courier.

More recently, Hazel had been working as a part-
time stenographer for Emerly, copying his work, here in
this apartment. This explained the adjoining workroom
and it occurred to Murdock that Hazel must have done
very well to furnish this apartment with such nice things.
It also occurred to him that Emerly, as her employer,
would most certainly be questioned about her death. On
impulse, but prompted by the thought that he had known

Emerly a long time, he moved into the workroom and picked up the telephone.

He could hear the distant buzzing after he had dialed his connection and it took a half minute or so to get an answer. When it came the voice was sleepy and tinged with irritation as Murdock identified himself.

"For God's sake," Emerly said. "Your guy called and gave me the message about the golf game around ten. I told him I didn't think I'd play... Do you know what time it is?"

"Yeah," Murdock said. "And this isn't about golf, George. It's about Hazel."

"Hazel? Hazel Franklin? What the devil has she done now?"

"She got herself killed," Murdock said and went on hurriedly to give a brief account of what had happened.

"You mean she was murdered?" Emerly said in slow amazement.

"Strangled, I think. With a stocking." He heard the other's shocked and inarticulate answer and he hurried on to explain that he had brought some pictures to the office and that he would be returning to Bayview in a half hour or so. "The reason I called was to break the news and ask if you wanted to go back with me."

"You mean now?"

"You don't have to," Murdock said. "But she worked for you and the police'll sure as hell question you. If you go down there now you can get the preliminaries over; you might even be able to tell them something that will help."

"Yeah," said Emerly. "They'll probably have someone here at the crack of dawn anyway... Yeah," he said.

"I'd like to go. Thanks for giving me the tip, kid."

"Be at the office as soon as you can," Murdock said. "And don't dawdle."

Putting the telephone aside he glanced over the room and inspected the swinging door which apparently led to the kitchen. There seemed to be no place here where a woman might keep a photograph album, so he went back to the living room and examined the desk. The already messed-up drawers yielded nothing that interested him, so he turned toward the short hallway opposite and to the bedroom at the end. This, too, was dark and he barged ahead, his mind occupied with problems of the past and instinct dulled by the false assumption that the apartment was empty.

It had not occurred to him that the one who had searched the desk might still be here. There had been no sound, no intuitive warning to prompt him to proceed with caution. There was none now as he took a step and halfturned to grope for a light switch.

The attack was as surprising as it was unexpected, and since he had no time to brace himself he was momentarily helpless when the man jumped him, springing from some place on the left and clamping an arm around his throat so that the crook of the elbow was notched securely beneath the point of his chin. All he knew at that instant was that the man was as tall as he was and had a muscular arm.

Before he could react his body was bent backward from the waist. At the same time his breath was cut off and he felt the crushing pressure against his Adam's apple. He tried to turn and could not. He remembered a trick he had learned during the war, but the man's body was pressed too close to his. He tried to hook with one elbow. When that didn't work he put both hands to the arm that imprisoned him and yanked at it; then slid a hand along a hairy wrist, feeling the watch there and trying again to break the grip.

The seconds lengthened agonizingly as they struggled, their weight shifting as Murdock moved and the man countered and kept his balance. He could hear the wheezing of breath in his ear as the man exerted himself, but his own breathing had stopped and his lungs were bursting and the blackness in front of his eyes began to explode with dancing red lights.

He knew he would lose consciousness shortly, and then, not panicking but calling forth some extra effort born of pain and desperation, he tore again at the wrist and let his weight sag against the arm. It did not free him but it made the other adjust his grip and this time when Murdock hooked his elbow he felt it sink into the flesh below the breastbone. He heard the sudden gasp and was encouraged. He kicked back, his heel biting into a shin, and hooked again with his elbow, and then his neck was free and he was pitching headfirst into the blackness as his adversary heaved him straight ahead.

The change in tactics was so sudden that Murdock never did get his balance. His weight was so far forward that when his leg struck the edge of the bed he pitched to the floor and landed on his hip. By then the door had slammed to make the darkness complete and when he started to rise he was still giddy and dropped to one knee.

There he stayed, sucking air into his lungs and trying to swallow, until the room steadied and he felt he could stand. Groping in the general direction of the door, he finally found the switch and snapped light into the room. In the hall he turned at once into the bathroom, ran some water, and cupped it in his hand so he could suck at it and ease the aching dryness in his throat. He still did not know whether the intruder had wanted to kill him or merely wanted to get away, and he did not speculate about it. He had come here with a definite idea in mind and now he went stubbornly back into the bedroom to continue his search.

The door on his right opened into a large closet wellfilled with dresses. There were two paper laundrybags in the center and one had had the front ripped out of it, disclosing the frock that still bore its laundry tag. The hatboxes on the shelf did not interest him, so he closed the door and turned to the dresser. He found what he wanted in the bottom drawer, a leather album partly covered by slips and nightgowns.

There were four photographs to the page and the third page held a good likeness of Hazel Franklin. She was posing on a dock with water behind her, and the man who stood close to her grinning at the camera was Paul Herrick, very handsome in slacks and a sport shirt that was open at the throat.

It was a glossy print. By proper cropping, a suitable reproduction of the woman could be made, and now, not bothering to look any further, Murdock slipped it from the corners which held it and closed the album. When he replaced it he turned the slips and gowns well back to get the album underneath; that was how he happened to see the letters which rested between two garments nearer the middle of the drawer.

For a moment he merely looked at them; then he reached, aware that the stationery was of good quality and that the handwriting was a man's. There were perhaps a dozen in all and when he flipped through them he saw that the handwriting was the same. The thought that they were both personal and private was corroborated by their hiding place and the fact that they were tied with a narrow silken ribbon.

Murdock had no intention of taking them. He had not even made up his mind whether he ought to read one or not when he heard the distant knocking at the door, a startling sound in all that stillness.

Not for an instant was there any doubt in his mind about that sound and he reacted swiftly, caring nothing at all about who, or why, but wanting only to get out, knowing if there was a back door he could make it and if there was none he could not.

The rap of his calf against the drawer closed it and he hurried out of the room and down the hall, the letters still in his hand though he was not aware of them. The knocking came again, vigorously this time, and as he reached for the light switch next to the door he could hear the muted voices beyond. Four steps took him into the workroom and his groping hands found the swinging door. He slapped through it to the kitchen, found another switch. He flipped it on and off and that brief glimpse told him there was a way out.

He said: "Ahh—" as he exhaled and then he was turning the key and opening the metal door and slipping onto the landing outside. A dim nightlight from somewhere above outlined the narrow stairwell and the metal treads that wound downward and he took them two at a time as his hand slid down the railing. At the bottom he noticed the letters for the first time and swore under his breath before he thrust them into his pocket.

The door opened into what seemed like an alley but when it closed again the blackness was complete until his eyes adjusted themselves and he could make out an opening to the street on his right. There was no light in the brick walls that rose canyon-like above him, no sound but the tap of his shoes and the rustle of his breathing. The side street was empty when he gained the walk. A taxi sped by at the corner and, more distantly, he heard the shifting gears as a heavy truck accelerated. At the intersection he stopped to glance along the street where his car was parked some fifty feet from the apartment entrance. Directly in front of this another car had nosed in toward the curb, its lights still on. From where he stood Murdock could not tell whether anyone was in it, so he approached cautiously, keeping to the curb side and the shadows of the other cars parked there.

The sedan that interested him was small, black, and unmarked. Only the extended radio antenna suggested it was a police vehicle and when he saw it was empty he moved close enough to see the license plate and be sure. After that he walked quickly on to his own car, climbed in and got it rolling.

CHAPTER 5

GEORGE EMERLY was waiting in the studio when Murdock walked in; so was Fred Berry, a smooth-faced youth who had recently come from a smaller newspaper in the western part of the state to work for the Courier.

"Where've you been?" Emerly said.

"I had to go out... Do you two know each other? George Emerly—Fred Berry."

They said hello and Berry said he had read some of Emerly's stuff, and Murdock asked if Klime was around. Berry said he had just left.

"Give me five minutes," Murdock said, "and I'll be ready."

He went out before anyone could reply, rode the elevator to the city room, and took the photograph of Hazel Franklin to the desk. He did not explain where he got it and no questions were asked. Long experience had convinced the editor that all photographers were a little nuts anyway. Nothing pleased them more than to produce hard-to-get pictures, but for some reason, apparently known only to other photographers, they became universally mysterious about sources and circumstances.

He nodded and put the print aside. "Good enough, Kent," he said. "We can use it in the final and we'll want it for Monday's editions if the story develops. Berry downstairs?"

Murdock said he was. "I know the chief at Bayview," he added. "I'll introduce Berry and he can come back on the train tomorrow."

Emerly was pacing the studio when Murdock returned. He was a tall, wiry man with a long, worry-lined face and thinning hair that had been sandy and was now mostly gray. The amber-rimmed glasses gave his

gray eyes a professorial look, and his brow wrinkled as
the eyes focused on Murdock.

"I brought my own car," he said, "because I don't
want to get stuck down there while you finish that golf
game. But I want to talk to you and—" He broke off and
glanced at the reporter. "You can drive, can't you, Berry?
How about you taking my car and I'll ride with Kent?"

"Sure," Berry said.

Murdock would have been ready to go if he hadn't
chosen that moment to put his hand in his pocket and be
reminded that he still had the packet of letters. Now, not
sure just what he should do with them, he told Emerly
and Berry he would meet them at the parking lot. When
they went out he stepped into his little office and snapped
on the light.

It took only a moment to slip one envelope out of the
ribbon, another to open it and glance at the sheet it
contained. Written in longhand, the letter started with
Dearest and ended With all my love, Paul. In between the
subject matter was both passionate and indiscreet, the
end result an expression of sentiment that a woman
might keep and a man might well regret.

Murdock replaced the letter and envelope as his mind
dwelt on the thought. He unlocked the center drawer of
the desk—his own private drawer—pushed the letters
toward the back and re-locked it. As he snapped off the
light he could not help wondering if, out of all the Pauls
in town, the writer could have been Paul Herrick. George
Emerly said very little until the suburbs were behind and
Murdock fed more gas to the car. His lanky frame was
jackknifed on the seat and his hat was tipped over his
eyes. Murdock did not prompt him and finally Emerly
stirred, flipped his cigarette out the lowered window, and
cleared his throat.

"I said I wanted to talk to you. It's kind of a long
story and the reason I came along is because I want some
advice. You get around. You know everybody. You know
some of the cops on Homicide and what makes them tick.

What I'm getting at is this: I don't think I'm going to get just a routine questioning. I think it'll be a lot more than that.

"For instance," he said, when Murdock made no comment, "the police are going to want to know all about Hazel—I mean unless they can tag someone right away and prove he killed her. They're going to check into her life and her past and her habits and who her friends were. Things like that."

"Probably," Murdock said, not yet knowing what Emerly was trying to prove.

"They'll check her bank account and when they do they'll find out I've been giving her a check for a hundred and a quarter a week for several months. They'll say:

'What the hell did she do for you to earn that kind of dough?' and I'll say: 'She did a little spare time copying.'"

He grunted softly. "They won't buy that so I'll tell 'em the twenty-five was for the copying and the hundred was for something else. That's why I said it was a long story. It goes back to Ted Franklin—and even before."

He was speaking of Franklin then and Murdock's thoughts went far back to recall the Ted Franklin who was working for the Courier and using his spare time trying to write short stories. He had been married to Hazel then, and the stories had never sold, and later, when Hazel had left him and gone to New York, he had sold off the apartment furniture and moved in with Emerly before he found a job with the news magazine that finally sent him to Hungary and his tragic death.

Emerly, who was much older and a confirmed bachelor, was a rewrite man, but he too had aspirations in the freelance field. He began by writing features for the Sunday magazine section at space rates and branched out into doing true crime stories and fact pieces. When he discovered he could make a living in this field he had quit the paper. Other markets had opened up for him and in the past few years he had been on his own, concentrating mostly on articles but selling an occasional piece of fiction. He spoke of this now as Murdock again tuned in his words.

"Ted wrote twenty-odd short stories while he was living with Hazel," he said, "but none of them sold. When he moved in with me he brought the originals and carbons with him. Every once in a while he'd submit one of them again, but they always came back with a rejection slip and he finally gave up. When he got the magazine job he left those old stories with me because they were too heavy to cart around and yet he couldn't bring himself to tear them up. He thought Hazel was divorcing him—and so did I—but as it turned out she never did.

"I thought about those stories when I learned he'd been killed, but I didn't actually read one for quite a while. I'd sold a couple of shorts of my own but never to a first-class market. I'd always had trouble with fiction and finally one day when I was knocking myself out trying to get an idea I read one of Ted's yarns. I could see then why no one would buy it. He just didn't know how to write the sort of thing a magazine would publish and yet the idea itself was damn good... Well, to keep this short, I took that idea and one of the characters and sat down and got to work. I didn't just rewrite it; I made a completely new story out of it. My agent liked it and so did Everyman's Magazine. They bought it for twelve hundred and fifty bucks, and asked for more."

He got another cigarette going and said: "I tried another and sold that for fifteen, and a third at the same price. But what was more important was that I got a feel for commercial fiction I'd never had before. I got confidence, I felt I knew how it should be done. I got an idea of my own and developed it and it went to the magazine for two grand, and then to television for three, and finally to the movies for thirty-five thousand, which I had to split with the guy who did the teleplay.

"When I couldn't get another idea of my own I tried another of Ted's and then, with some dough to coast on, I tried a book. It'll be out in a couple of weeks and the Digest Book Club is taking it and there's a possibility of a movie sale... But the thing to bear in mind is that Ted was an orphan. I thought he was divorced. He had no heirs. The stories I used weren't mine, but whose were they? They were worthless as they were, and if he'd been alive we could have split fifty-fifty."

"There hadn't been any divorce?" Murdock said.

"No."

"Hazel had copied them originally. She read one of them somewhere or saw one on TV and remembered."

"Right. And she's a very greedy dame. She'd been working in New York as a public stenographer and she came running with her little hand out. And the hell of it was, she had me. There'd been no divorce and she'd really inherited those old stories. So after we'd screamed at each other for a while we made a deal. On the stories I'd used and sold she was to get half. When we added things up I didn't have enough to give her half so I wrote a check for twenty-five hundred and agreed to give her a hundred a week on account."

He cleared his throat and said: "But I wouldn't go for that deal on the stories that were left, the ones I hadn't used. They weren't worth a dime in their present shape and she knew it. I said I could get along without them now; I told her to take them and clear out, but she knew better than that. I admitted I might be able to use some of them, but it would still be a lot of work and if she wanted to settle for twenty-five per cent—after commission—okay; otherwise, no deal... She took it. We signed an agreement."

"I saw it," Murdock said.

For another quarter of a mile there was no sound but the hum of the motor. He kept his eyes on the road but he could see Emerly turn toward him and feel the intensity of his gaze.

"You what? How could you?"

"I stopped by her apartment tonight," Murdock said, and then he was explaining why he had gone there and how he had entered. He did not mention the man who jumped him, or speak of the letters, but he said it was obvious that someone had been there before him.

"I don't know what the guy was looking for, but the desk had been searched and this agreement was on the floor with some other papers."

After a while Emerly said: "Well, I'll be damned. . . . Yeah. She's got one copy and I've got the other."

"So what're you worried about?"

"Well—I mean—the cops check with the bank and they find out I paid her twenty-five hundred and then a hundred and twenty-five a week for twenty-five bucks worth of work—to show you how suspicious she is, she picks up my morning's work every day and copies it to make sure I don't slip a fast one over on her—and the cops'll say this dame has got her hooks in you, Emerly. Maybe that's a motive for murder."

Murdock grunted and said: "You've got too much imagination. You can explain those payments and you have the stories and records to prove it. Where's the strain?"

"The thing to do is tell them the truth?"

"Certainly."

"I understand she has a brother," Emerly said. "I suppose he'd inherit whatever she has. The contract was with Hazel, but I suppose I could pay him the cut if I use any more of Ted's stories."

"Probably," Murdock said. "But you can get a legal opinion on that."

"Yeah. Well—" Emerly sat up and adjusted his hat, his voice suddenly relieved. "I guess that's okay then. This thing sort of knocked me over and my conscience was bothering me because I really did use some stories that weren't mine. I wouldn't even have thought of it if I'd known anyone could ever claim them."

"Naturally you wouldn't," Murdock said.

"Well, that's all right then," Emerly said. "And thanks for listening. I feel better already."

CHAPTER 6

THE BAYVIEW POLICE STATION was a one-story brick building with a garage and four seldom used cells in the basement and four rooms upstairs—a waiting room with the booking desk, an office for the chief, a detention room, and a recreation room with lockers and a shower in the rear. The police force consisted of five men, including Nickerson, the chief, and one of these was talking to Berry when Murdock and Emerly entered. Charlie Lane sat by himself near one wall. Murdock walked over to him.

"How'd it go?"

"Okay."

"Charlie—this is George Emerly—Charlie Lane... George plays a little golf once in a while."

"I'm a hacker, Charlie," Emerly said as he shook hands. "You got a lot of company."

The uniformed officer had been watching this and now he stepped up.

"You're Murdock, aren't you? The chief's waiting for you."

"Is he sore?"

"A little."

Murdock glanced again at Charlie. "Are you through or just waiting?"

"I don't know. They said to wait."

"I'll give you a lift back to the motel when I'm finished with the chief." He looked at the officer. "Anyone with him?"

"Lieutenant Carlin of the state police." He walked over to a door, knocked, stuck his head in. "Murdock's here."

"Get him in here," a voice said.

Murdock nodded to Emerly and led the way into the office. The man who scowled up at him from behind the desk was chunky and middle-aged, his bald head suntanned, his heavy face florid.

"A fine thing," he said irritably. "If I didn't know you I'd have asked the Boston police to pick you up and hold you."

"Didn't Charlie Lane tell you why I took off?"

"Sure he told me."

"I came back, didn't I? I didn't hold you up, did I?"

He grinned, knowing that the chief was not really annoyed but understanding that he had to complain about such unorthodox conduct. "I brought a reporter back with me," he said. "Treat him right and he'll put your name in the papers."

"Phuie," said Nickerson. "Sit down. This is Lieutenant Carlin."

Carlin nodded, a lean-bodied man in sport coat and slacks. About forty, Murdock thought, with shrewd, expressionless blue eyes and light-brown hair that had been recently cut and seemed a bit too short.

Murdock said: "Hello, Lieutenant," and introduced Emerly. "I got him out of bed and brought him along because I thought he might be able to help."

"We could use some," Carlin said. "You knew her, Mr. Emerly?"

Emerly sat down and explained what Hazel Franklin had done for him.

"How well did you know her?"

"Well—I saw her nearly every day for a few minutes."

"But just for business reasons, huh? No emotional problem there?"

"Good God, no I" Emerly laughed shortly. "I'm twenty years older than she was and I don't make the kind of money that would interest her. I'm a writer."

"Money was important to her, is that it?"

"Very."

"So who was she interested in?"

Emerly thought it over. He glanced at Murdock and his brows bunched above the amber-rimmed glasses. Finally he said:

"She had quite a few dates with Carl Darrow."

"I know him," Nickerson said to Carlin. "He owns part of the Blue Heron."

"Who else?" Carlin said.

Emerly gestured with one hand. "I wasn't interested in her love life, Lieutenant. I only saw her a few minutes each day. I think she dated quite a few guys on and off. She was the kind of woman that wouldn't want to sit home every night."

"Who, specifically, besides Darrow," said Carlin, still pressing.

"I heard she knew a man by the name of Paul Herrick pretty well, but that was a while back and anyway you couldn't prove it by me. I don't even remember where I heard it."

Nickerson made some notes on a pad. "Herrick's a piano player," he said to Carlin. "Has the orchestra at the Heron. Or did. I understand they closed last night... You want to go over exactly how you found her and what you did, Kent?"

Murdock shifted in his chair and stretched his legs. The story he told was accurate but not all inclusive. Because he did not think it pertinent, he made no mention of the accident he had photographed or the blonde Lucille or the filmholders he had lost.

Nickerson massaged his nose. "When you had those drinks at the Heron did you happen to see Carl Darrow?"

"Once."

"When?"

"About eleven thirty or so."

"What was he doing?"

"Talking to Herrick."

"You didn't see Darrow before that?" Carlin asked.

Murdock shook his head and digressed. "What does the medical examiner say about when she was killed?"

"Not much," Carlin said dryly. "First he said anywhere from seven thirty to nine thirty. When we pointed out the woman didn't register until five after eight he made it from then until nine thirty. Maybe later he can pin it down a bit more, but not now."

He leaned forward to examine some notes at the end of the desk. "Registered at 8:05. Used her right name but a phony license number. We checked it. Belongs to a retired railroad man up in Stoneham."

"So we figure it wasn't her car," Nickerson said. "Must have belonged to a boyfriend who was being careful, though we're not sure why. Charlie Lane says there was a man in that car but he didn't get a good look at him, and you say there never was a car parked next to that particular unit, not while you were there."

"Mr. Emerly." Carlin tipped his head and studied the writer. "You saw Hazel Franklin nearly every day. Did she have any jewelry? Any rings? A wrist watch—anything like that?"

Emerly blinked pale-gray eyes and nodded slightly.

"Yes," he said, "she did. Two rings and a wrist watch."

"Describe them, please."

"Well—one ring was a solitaire."

"Big?"

"Not especially."

"Left hand?"

"Right... She had the other on the little finger of the left hand. A fancier job. What you'd call a cocktail ring, I think. A sapphire—or what looked like one—with some small diamonds around it."

Carlin exchanged glances with the chief and his eyes seemed to brighten with new interest.

"What about the watch?"

"Platinum studded with diamonds. It looked expensive."

Carlin said: "Okay," and leaned back, and Nickerson said:

"The M.E. noticed the marks on her fingers—"

"She didn't have any rings when I saw her," Murdock cut in.

"—and said it looked like she'd been wearing two rings recently. Also there was a faint mark on the left wrist that made him curious."

"Before you leave," Carlin said to Emerly, "we'll want a full description—as close as you can make it anyway. Because it just might be that those pieces'll give us a motive... There was a mink stole in the closet and a twenty-dollar bill in her wallet."

"It don't look like a premeditated job," Nickerson added.

"Some guy could have walked in on her. If she started to scream he could've panicked and used that stocking, not meaning to kill her, not realizing what he was doing until it was too late."

Murdock considered the premise, finding an objection or two but not voicing them.

"Or it could have been the boyfriend," Carlin said. "He was pretty cagey about keeping his identity covered. If they had a row and she blew her top the guy could have grabbed her... What kind of woman was she, Mr. Emerly?"

"Difficult."

"Hard to get along with?"

"I thought so."

"If it was the boyfriend," Murdock said, "why steal the jewelry?"

"Maybe this guy bought some of it and figured we could trace it to him... Just for the record, where were you last night, Mr. Emerly?"

There had been no hesitation, no change in inflection, and the question caught Emerly off guard. He stared, started to laugh, and thought better of it. He wet his lips and shrugged one shoulder.

"Home."

"Alone?"

"I'm afraid so, Lieutenant."

"I phoned him at around seven thirty," Murdock said. "The line was busy, so I left word for one of my photographers to call him later."

He spoke of the message and Emerly said:

"I talked to the fellow about ten o'clock."

"Okay." Carlin pursed his lips and glanced again at the chief. "I guess that does it for now. What're your plans for tomorrow?" he said, glancing at Murdock and Emerly.

"Kent says he's got an extra bed in his room," Emerly replied. "I can stay around until you're through with me."

"I'm playing golf." Murdock glanced at his watch and saw that it was four fifteen. "I hope."

"Stop in here before you go back to the city," Nickerson said.

Murdock stood and stretched. "Okay to take Charlie Lane back to the motel with me?"

Nickerson nodded; then he grinned. "Is Charlie going to caddy for you? . . . What a character," he said. "He breaks his back out on a golf course until he's a couple of hundred ahead and then goes to the track and has to hitch-hike back. The last I heard he was flat again."

Murdock led the way to the front room and gave Charlie Lane the word. He asked Berry if he wanted to go to the motel and see if there was a room, but Berry said he'd stick around.

"I want to get a statement from the chief and the lieutenant," he said. "There's a fairly early train out of here and I'll try to be on it."

He handed Emerly the keys to his car and Emerly said he would follow Murdock to the motel. When they got started Murdock turned to Charlie and asked if he was still game to caddy.

"Sure," said Charlie. "I need the dough."

"When does that lunchroom open?"

"Seven on Sunday."

"If I'm not in there by seven thirty, bang on the door."

CHAPTER 7

IT TOOK A KNOCK to rouse Murdock, but he came awake instantly and went to the door to thank Charlie Lane. In the other bed Emerly was snoring softly, and Murdock went into the bath to brush his teeth and examine his chin. Deciding he could postpone his shave until he returned after his golf, he donned a pair of lightweight slacks and a navy polo shirt. When he had put on a sweater he took his golf shoes and sox from the leather duffel bag, substituting his soiled shirt, tie, and the odds and ends on the dresser top.

He got out without waking Emerly and backed his car from the port, pleased that it was going to be a fine day for golf, with a slightly overcast sky and very little breeze. He had juice, bacon and eggs, toast and coffee in the lunchroom, and Charlie was waiting when he came into the lobby... Doctor Markey was swinging a club when Murdock walked up to the pro shop at Catansett and he called out to say he had registered and paid the green fees for both.

The two men usually played three or four times a summer, and their games were close enough so that there was never any strokes given or any adjusting on the tenth tee. Anything under ninety was a satisfactory game for either, and now when Markey said: "Same game?" Murdock said:

"Yeah. A buck each way and press on the back nine if we want to."

The foursome that was gathering on the first tee told them to go through and they hurried a bit, which didn't do their game any good. At the end of four holes Murdock, with a double bogie and three bogies, was one down.

"You ain't thinkin'," Charlie said on the fifth fairway, after Murdock had duck-hooked his drive. "You quit on that one."

"I won't quit on the next one," Murdock said. "I'll follow through if it kills me."

When he got to his ball he took a three-wood. He concentrated on following through. What came forth was a half-top that ran well because the ground was hard, but was badly hit.

"I followed through," he said with some belligerence.

"Sure," said Charlie, "but when you hit it your head was gone. Stay with it. Cet your hands into the shot."

Murdock was two down with a forty-six at the end of nine and Markey asked if he wanted to press the bet. "Start me one up?" Murdock said.

"I'll start you nothing."

"That's what I thought," Murdock said. "Okay, I press."

He played better after the eleventh when Charlie gave him one more piece of advice after he had dug into a shot.

"You lunged at it," Charlie said, and Murdock knew exactly what he meant. He had pivoted properly, but instead of unwinding on the way down he had shifted his body laterally. Remembering this, he improved at once and was again reminded of how helpful Charlie could be as a caddy.

Seldom offering advice unless asked for it, this advice was never technical when it came. Succinct and graphic, it was always to the point, and even as Murdock began to concentrate on his shots his mind considered the man again as he walked the fairways.

Although Charlie had a married son, a graduate engineer now living with his wife and two children, somewhere in southern California, he still seemed to have but two interests—golf and horses. Yet even in golf he seemed content to caddy, following the sun to Florida from October to May and then moving north again, with stops in the Carolinas if his money ran out. If there was any sort of tournament in this part of the state Charlie was there, usually carrying for one of the leading professionals, most of whom knew him. It was the same in Florida, but even though he made good money there the race tracks got it in the end. He had once won twelve hundred dollars in an afternoon and the hope of repeating this killing had become a complex that lured him on. It embarrassed him not at all to admit that the caddies at some Florida club had to take up a collection to buy him a bus ticket north one spring when his luck had turned somewhat worse than usual. Now, because Murdock liked the man, and knew of no one who didn't, he said:

"You can't keep caddying forever, Charlie."

"I know it."

"Why don't you live out near your son? They've got golf courses out there."

"Lots of 'em. I did go out one winter. They've got a room for me in their house, got its own entrance. Everything's nice too, but—I don't know. My daughter-in-law don't think much of the races and neither of 'em like the idea of me caddyin'."

"Couldn't you get a job as an assistant pro somewhere?"

"Maybe I will some day."

"How long since you've played?"

"A long time. I hit a few now and then."

"Are you going south again?"

"Sure. Maybe a little early this year. Soon as I collect my get-away money."

Markey, who had come over to get a club and heard them talking, said: "Hey. No coaching."

"He's my caddy too," Murdock said. "And I need it. How do we stand?"

"Even on this side."

Moving off the seventeenth tee Murdock was on the left side of the fairway again and now, his mind going back to the night before, he said:

"You know a girl named Lucille Dunn over at the Blue Heron?"

"I know who she is," Charlie said. "Blonde? Stacked? Yeah, a nice kid."

"You know Carl Darrow too, don't you?"

"A little."

"Did you ever see him around with the blonde?"

"No."

"Have you seen him with the woman who was killed?"

Charlie trudged along a silent moment, his body bent under the weight of the two bags, his head down.

"Seems like I have," he said finally.

"At the motel?"

"No. Only at the club. I stop in sometimes to get a snort. I saw 'em eating dinner a couple of times."

"Do you know his wife?"

"I've seen her. But not this summer. Last year, yes."

"Where does he stay when he's down here?"

"You know that motel a couple of miles beyond the club? Well, I understand he leases a couple of rooms with a kitchen there."

At the eighteenth tee the match was still even on this side and Markey, up first, sliced into the woods. Murdock said he knew the doctor would crack under pressure, and Markey defied him to take advantage of the opening.

Murdock did, smacking one straight down the middle about two hundred and twenty yards.

"I hit that one," he said proudly.

"It's about your first," Charlie said. "You ought to do it every time."

They waited down the fairway for Markey to chip out and Murdock laughed when he saw the doctor's third catch a trap. He had about a hundred and fifty yards left and he glanced at the club Charlie handed him.

"I'll never make it with a five-iron," he said.

"Hit it," said Charlie. "Get your hands in and stay with the shot and you'll be right up by the stick."

Murdock hit it right. He could tell by the feel, and they both watched the ball climb and then drop on the apron and kick to within fifteen feet of the pin. Murdock felt so good he took out another ball and dropped it. He handed Charlie the club.

"You hit one."

"Ahh—I'm out of practice."

"Hit it—"

Charlie cocked an eye at him and his sunburned face warped in a grin. He put away the five-iron and took out a seven. He balanced the club as he adjusted his grip, put the head down behind the ball, and placed his feet. He gave a small forward press and came back in a compact, all-in-one-piece swing, a little flat because his was a natural, imitative swing picked up as a boy. His hand action was crisp and there was no strain as the ball clicked and the hand-sized divot flew. He plunked the club back into the bag Murdock was holding while the ball was still in the air and together they watched it hit about three feet inside Murdock's shot, bounce six feet toward the pin, and then bite and kick back another foot.

"Okay?" he said as he started off.

Murdock sighed and shook his head. "It'll do," he said, with mock indifference. "It's a little short—"

"That's what I was thinking. Leaves me about a five-footer."

Markey reached the apron from the trap and putted up about three feet from the pin. Murdock took his putter and Charlie said: "Look it over good. You need this."

Murdock knew he could three-putt and still win this side and break even with the pressed bet, but he studied the line thoroughly and concentrated on keeping his head still. He hit it firmly and knew it was in all the way. Charlie nodded his approval. "The bird gave you an eighty-nine."

Markey picked up and said Murdock was a lucky stiff and how about a drink. Murdock said he'd have a quick one and Markey could buy it because of the birdie, and

now he let the doctor move on ahead and stayed with
Charlie. Markey had paid the green fee and he would pay
the caddy, but he didn't want Markey to know he was
going to give Charlie ten dollars. Normally at this club six
would have been plenty but he had always felt that
Charlie's advice was worth something extra and the
eighty-nine had made the round for him.

He waited until Charlie put his bag in the rear deck
of his car and then handed him two five-dollar bills.
Charlie's eyes opened appreciatively as he accepted the
money.

"Thank you," he said.

"You're a big help," Murdock said.

"Any time." Charlie took some bills from his pocket
and added the two fives. When Murdock noticed that the
caddy already had two or three twenties to go with the
fives, he nearly said: "You've already got a start on that
get-away money."

What stopped him was a new thought that was
instantly disturbing. By some odd contortion of the brain
he remembered a statement Chief Nickerson had made
earlier that morning: that Charlie had very recently been
flat broke. It had also been said that the wallet in Hazel
Franklin's pocketbook had contained a single twenty-
dollar bill. Yet the night before, when Murdock had
examined that wallet as he looked for some identification,
he had distinctly seen at least three or four bills of the
same denomination.

He glanced at Charlie as he pocketed the money, as if
he expected the round, sunburned face to supply some
clue. There was certainly time for the man to have taken
those bills while he waited for the police, but although
Murdock realized this he tried to dismiss the thought
because he was ashamed of it. Charlie was no thief. If he
found some bills lying around unclaimed he might take
them—

Again he tried to erase the supposition. He closed the
rear deck and said he'd give Charlie a ride if he would

wait until he had a quick drink with Doctor Markey. Even then, as he turned toward the clubhouse, his dark eyes were troubled and his thoughts continued to nag him.

CHAPTER 8

IT WAS a quarter of three when Kent Murdock parked his car beside the police station in Bayview. There had been a note from George Emerly at the motel saying that the writer had gone back to the city, and when Murdock had shaved and showered, he put on a clean polo shirt, packed his bags, and loaded his car. He had stopped for a sandwich and a beer at a near-by restaurant and now, as he strode through the front room of the station house, a strange policeman asked what he wanted.

"The chief asked me to stop in."

"There's somebody with him."

"I'll just check anyway," Murdock said, not slowing down, and then he had knocked once and opened the door to the private office. "Okay to come in?"

Nickerson frowned at the interruption but Lieutenant Carlin just looked, his face revealing nothing, his slouched body unmoving. Across the desk from the chief was a man Murdock recognized but did not know: the district attorney, a graying man of forty or so with a neat and well-fed look and dark-rimmed glasses. Off to one side and sitting by himself was Paul Herrick.

"You said to stop in," Murdock added quickly, wanting to stay and listen.

"Yeah." Nickerson gave the red nose a rub and glanced at the district attorney. "All right," he said with some reluctance. "But nothing you get here is for publication.

. . . Do you know our district attorney—Mr. O'Brien?"

Murdock said hello and found a chair. O'Brien conquered his initial annoyance and consulted the papers on the desk, turning finally to Herrick.

"Getting back to Mrs. Franklin," he said. "You were very friendly at one time, but not recently. This period when you were friendly—was this in Boston?"

"No, New York. I had a trio down there last winter and spring."

"She came to Boston in April?"

"Around there."

"What about you?"

"I think it was May," Herrick said. "I opened at the Heron June fifteenth and for a couple of weeks before that I wasn't working."

"So when did this affair end?"

Herrick shifted in his chair, and his big hands were restless as they picked at the crease in his slacks and then raked his short brown hair. The light-brown eyes were truculent, but he did not object to O'Brien's phrasing.

"Soon after she came to Boston," he said.

"You haven't seen her lately? When, exactly, did you see her last?"

Herrick hesitated over the question. He hunched both shoulders, let them fall. "Last week, I guess. I ran into her somewhere, I don't remember now."

O'Brien said: "Hmmm. Now about last night. From about seven until eight thirty you were eating dinner at the Heron."

"That checks out," Nickerson said. "Except for a phone call some time after eight the waiter says he was eating."

"When did you start to play?"

"Around nine thirty."

"So what did you do between eight thirty and nine thirty?"

"Nothing."

"I beg your pardon."

"I was around," Herrick said woodenly. "I don't know what I was doing. I was in my room part of the time—in that cottage out back. There are seven or eight rooms for some of the help. Two of the boys in the band stay there too; the married ones live where they want to."

Murdock considered the answer and knew that part of it was faulty. He had seen Herrick drive out of the motel somewhere around nine thirty, but there had only been an instantaneous glance and he was not ready to swear that it was Herrick. Until he was more certain it seemed best to say nothing at all.

But he could not help thinking about the letters he had taken from Hazel Franklin's apartment. There was no way of telling at the moment whether Herrick was the Paul who had written them, but he recalled the man's story about the girl he was to marry in another month, and he understood how much trouble such letters could stir up if Herrick had sent them. Those letters bothered Murdock. He had not meant to take them. He was sorry he had done so because they had put him in an untenable position. He could not mention them without admitting he had entered that apartment unlawfully, and he could not bring himself to jeopardize Herrick's position until he could be sure the man had written them.

There was, however, one more thing he remembered. When he had upset Hazel Franklin's bag he had enumerated its contents and one thing had been missing. Keys.

Suppose Herrick had killed the woman because of those letters or some threat she had made to use them, either maliciously or for the purpose of extortion. Herrick would have had to get them back. He would certainly have taken the key to her apartment, and if this was the case it seemed likely that he was the man who had jumped Murdock in the darkened bedroom before his search had been completed.

The more Murdock considered the problem the more confused and unhappy he became, and now he forced his mind back to the moment and picked up the conversation as O'Brien tried to find out where Herrick had gone after he quit playing the piano at eleven forty.

"I had a date," Herrick was saying. "Let's leave it that way."

A knock prevented O'Brien from pursuing the subject, and the uniformed officer stuck his head inside to announce that Carl Darrow had arrived.

"Tell him to wait a minute," Nickerson said. "You got anything else on your mind for him?" he said to Carlin with a nod to indicate Herrick.

Carlin shook his head and remained mute. O'Brien pushed back his chair.

"All right, Mr. Herrick," he said. "Be here at nine tomorrow morning. We'll want a formal statement. When we get it typed up you can sign it."

Herrick stood, his tanned face tight and his gaze fixed straight ahead. Not once had he actually looked at Murdock, and as he walked out without a word, Nickerson rose and followed him to the doorway to call Carl Darrow. Darrow was a solid-looking man in his late forties, thick through the chest but carrying very little fat. His thinning dark hair held only a suggestion of gray above the tanned, boxlike face and his eyes seemed almost black beneath the straight strong brows. His manner was reserved as he was introduced and invited to sit down, his tan gabardine suit had an expensive sheen, and in his ruggedly masculine way he had an air about him that was both distinguished, intelligent, and, at the moment, unworried. Speaking to no one in particular, he said:

"Before we get started on this, do I need a lawyer?"

"Not unless you'd be more comfortable that way," O'Brien said dryly.

"No stenographer?"

"We're saving that for tomorrow. All we want from you now is the answers to a few questions and a little co-operation... You know what happened last night at the Pine Grove Motel?"

Darrow leaned back and crossed his knees. "Yes."

"Were you there at any time yesterday?"

"No."

"You still have an interest in the Blue Heron?'"

"I do."

"You were seen there last night about eleven thirty or a few minutes later. We'd like to know where you were before that?"

"How long before that?"

"All evening."

"Home. At my apartment."

"Alone?"

"Right. I was working on some papers."

O'Brien hesitated. As he drummed his fingers absently on the desk top, Carlin spoke.

"Where'd you have dinner, Mr. Darrow?"

"I didn't eat until I got to the club. I'd had a late lunch and I was busy."

"Is there any way you can prove you were in Boston?"

Darrow cleared his throat. There was a faint huskiness in his voice but it remained low-pitched and its oadence was flat and expressionless. He'd had, in former years, some experience with police methods and investigations, and Murdock, thinking again of the man's past, recalled the prison term he had once served.

The charge had been manslaughter when Darrow had killed a man in a fight over Darrow's first wife. This had happened twenty years ago and because of the circumstances he had served but four years and some months before being paroled. Even then Darrow had been working his way up in certain rackets—principally laundry and trucking—but though he had been picked up for questioning from time to time there had been no more arrests. Much of what Murdock knew could be attributed to rumor, but it was understood that Darrow had become moderately wealthy and that during the past five or six years he had retired from such activities and invested his money, and wisely, in Boston and Miami real estate. He had married again five years ago... Murdock held the thought as the man answered.

"I can tell you this, Lieutenant. I phoned my attorney about nine o'clock." He gave the lawyer's name and address and said: "I asked him to get some figures ready for me. He crabbed a bit because he had a bridge game scheduled, but he finally agreed. I picked the information up at his house at ten o'clock. Then I drove down here."

"Any particular reason why?" O'Brien asked.

"Because we were closing up the club last night. I had to pay off and get the books and records."

O'Brien shuffled some more papers. "You knew Mrs. Franklin?"

"I did."

"How well?"

Darrow tipped one hand. "I've been taking her around quite a bit."

O'Brien thought it over and then digressed. "I told you in the beginning that this session is more or less informal. We're after information and the Boston authorities are helping us get it. I have an idea they'll come up with a pretty good line on some phases of your private life, but you're under no compulsion to answer such questions now."

Darrow uncrossed his knees and allowed himself a thin smile. "Go ahead and try me," he said in his husky way. "I'll tell you when to stop."

Lieutenant Carlin, who had been letting O'Brien carry the ball for the most part, narrowed his gaze slightly and his resentment at Darrow's attitude began to show.

"Look," he said bluntly. "This is murder, and it could be that you're a material witness until you can prove different. As such we can hold you right now."

"Not for long."

"Being Sunday would help," Carlin said. "We could spoil the rest of the day for you and most of tomorrow."

"All right, Sam." O'Brien lifted his hand and considered Darrow again. "I'm sure Mr. Darrow wants to co-operate.

. . . You're a married man, aren't you?" he added quickly.

"Was Mrs. Darrow at your apartment last night?"

"She's in Florida."

"Since when?"

"Since June."

"Oh? Rather warm down there this time of year, isn't it?"

"That's what I told her," Darrow said, the small smile constant now but holding no warmth. "She thought she'd like to go down there for a divorce."

"Because of Mrs. Franklin?"

"That could have been part of it. There were other things."

The word divorce sent Murdock's thoughts off on another tangent and he wondered what Hazel Franklin had that could infatuate men like Herrick and Darrow. For Herrick was big and handsome; he had an attractive personality and a reasonably good education. In his business he was exposed to all kinds of women, and certainly attractive ones would not be hard to find.

Darrow, with the rough edges worn off by a growing affluence, and with his association with the rackets behind him, had a certain aura of success about him and the money to indulge his whims. In addition he had a wife who by Murdock's standards was both handsome and desirable. He did not know her but he had seen her from time to time, and it was hard now to understand the man's apparent preference for Hazel Franklin.

Not that Hazel was unattractive; quite the contrary. As a typist in the business office of the Courier before she married, she had been a small but seductively rounded girl, vivacious and gregarious. She had dated a half dozen men before settling on Ted Franklin. That she was selfish and demanding was soon demonstrated after the honeymoon, but it was not until she left Franklin that he recited chapter and verse to Murdock one night when he'd had too much to drink. Recalling the last time he had seen her, Murdock knew that she was still a good-looking woman, not pretty, but somehow exciting, a little bold, with a unique but definite air of sexiness about her, an almost decadent quality that defied analysis but was somehow reflected in the lines of her face, the movements of her body, the challenging look in her eyes. Whatever the allure, she had clearly exerted it on Darrow, who had seen enough of life to know what he was doing and was now answering a question O'Brien had put to him.

"When did I see Hazel last?" He considered a moment.

"Late yesterday afternoon."

"Where?"

"At her place."

"Did you know she was coming to the motel?" O'Brien watched Darrow shake his head. "Well, what did you talk about?"

"This and that. I told her I was driving down here last night and asked if she wanted to come. She said no. She said she'd see me Monday."

"Who else was she seeing?"

"Nobody that I know of."

O'Brien refused to buy the statement. His pained expression and the note of irritation in his voice said so.

"You've been around quite a while, Mr. Darrow," he said, enunciating with some care. "You spent a lot of time and probably considerable money on Mrs. Franklin... Now we know she arrived at the motel with a man around eight o'clock last night. You say it wasn't you."

"That's right."

"And you're trying to tell us that you have no idea who that man might be."

"I am telling you."

An abrupt curse punctuated the sentence. It came from Carlin and his tone was contemptuous when he spoke.

"You know what I think, Darrow? I think you're a liar."

"Why don't you try to prove it, Lieutenant?"

"Don't think we won't," Carlin said.

Darrow stood and looked at O'Brien. "You asked for some co-operation and you got it. If you want to argue you can do it with my lawyer."

"Then you'd better call him," Carlin said. "Because you're due here at nine in the morning."

"Think it over," O'Brien said. "Maybe you'll want to change your mind before morning, but either way what you say then will be for the record."

"Maybe I won't say a damn thing in the morning," Darrow said. "That's my privilege, isn't it?" He moved over to the door. "Unless you want to make your pinch now, I'll shove off."

Carlin began to swear anew when the door closed.

O'Brien looked perturbed as he collected his papers.

Nickerson, who had followed the investigation in silence, made only one comment.

"Sure, he's lying. The hell of it is we got to prove it."

Murdock pulled himself erect. When O'Brien asked if there was anything he would like to add, Murdock said no, and O'Brien reminded him that what he had heard was confidential and to keep it that way.

When Murdock went back to his car he decided to pay a final visit to the Blue Heron before going back to the city. He did not try to rationalize the impulse, but presently he found himself thinking again of the blonde Lucille Dunn, not because he had an idea that she had anything to do with the murder but simply because he wanted to see her. She had intrigued him last night, and he was curious to know what she was like when she wasn't working. There was a chance that he might still get some explanation for the trick she had played on him, and as he explored the possibility he remembered something that had long been dormant in his mind.

He had taken three pictures of that accident last night.

She had stolen the filmholder which held two of them, and the films had later been developed and destroyed.

But there was a third exposure—the first he had taken—and it remained where he had put it when he came to the motel: in the leather duffel bag. There would be time enough to develop this picture when he got back to the office; meanwhile there remained the interesting enigma of the girl.

The Blue Heron seemed deserted when he swung into the parking lot and eased his car round the end of the building. The windows were shuttered, the sign which spoke of charcoal-broiled steaks and broiled live lobsters had been removed, and it was not until he reached the rear that he saw the stack of shutters leaning against a side window.

The two bouncers who had manhandled him so neatly the night before looked different by daylight. Both wore tight blue jeans that were faded and paint-stained, and, though the afternoon was cool, T-shirts that molded nicely the muscles of their torsos. They looked younger now and less formidable. They grinned when they saw him get out of the car and start toward them, and it occurred to him that they should be playing professional football somewhere, for Felix had the height and weight of a tackle and Nate moved with the easy co-ordination of a halfback.

"Hi, chum," they said, and reached down into the grass to pick up the beer cans they had punctured. They each took a swallow. "You want a beer?"

"No, thanks," Murdock said.

"You bought last night," Felix said.

"So you got one comin'," added Nate. "There's some whisky around if you'd like a shot."

They leaned against the side of the cottage, their eyes amused as he shook his head.

"You're not sore, hunh?" Felix said.

"Why should I be?"

"That's the attitude we like to see," Nate said. "What's on your mind?"

"I was looking for Lucille."

"Gone," said Felix.

"So's her roommate," said Nate.

"Roommate?"

"The little doll—"

"—that took pictures."

"Everybody's gone," Felix said.

"Everybody but us flunkies," said Nate as he tossed the empty can aside.

"Boston?" Murdock asked.

"Yep," they said. "The big city."

"Do you know where I could find her?"

The smiles went away and the eyes grew speculative.

"You figure to give her any trouble?" Felix asked softly.

"Not me," Murdock said. "If she complains you can always look me up at the Courier"

They considered the remark as they exchanged glances. Finally Nate shrugged and reached for another shutter.

"You could try the Hotel Lynn," he said. "Just take it easy... Come on, big man," he said to Felix. "Let's wrestle another one of these."

Felix reached for the other end of the shutter. "So long, Mac," he said. "Say hello to Lucille for us."

"But keep it nice," said Nate. "Keep loose... We'll see you around."

CHAPTER 9

THE LONE OCCUPANT of the studio when Murdock walked in in the early evening was a youth by the name of Phil Terry, a cocky, rusty-haired newcomer to the staff who was determined to become the best photographer in the city. Murdock had stopped for a drink and dinner on the way up and he also had the filmholder which had been in the duffel bag. Now he said hello to Terry and went along the narrow corridor to one of the darkroom cubicles.

Of the two films in the holder, the first had no significance and had been taken Saturday morning when Murdock was on his way to work. A certain combination of light and shadow on the river had caught his eye, and because the pictorial quality pleased him he had stopped to capture the scene for himself. Now he developed this along with the accident shot and brought the negatives back to the printing-room tank. While he let them fix for a few minutes he went into his office and called police headquarters.

A sergeant he knew told him that Lieutenant Bacon had been assigned to cover this end of the Bayview case and this pleased Murdock—he had known Bacon for many years and had, on occasion, worked rather closely with him—until he asked himself why he should care who had the case.

He did not know who had killed Hazel Franklin. He was involved to the extent that he had helped find the body, but aside from a normal curiosity it made no difference to him who the guilty person was. Given a little time and the proper breaks the police would make an arrest and he, Murdock, might have to be a witness, but at the moment there was little point in worrying about the future.

. . . Except for one thing that finally became the focus of his thoughts.

What about the letters he had taken from Hazel Franklin's apartment and which were now locked in the center drawer of the desk?

He unlocked this drawer now. He turned the packet of letters over in his hands, his dark brows bunching and his gaze concerned as he kept asking himself two questions:

Should he turn them over to the police and involve himself in additional explanations? Or should he return them to Paul Herrick?

It took him quite a while to reach a decision. Even when it came it was most unsatisfactory. He was annoyed with himself for having taken the letters in the first place, even though the act had been unconscious rather than deliberate.

The point was—he had them. He was afraid to destroy them. And so he decided to wait further developments. If the police could build up sufficient evidence to charge Herrick with murder, he could go to Bacon and tell the truth. If, on the other hand, the police could find a more likely suspect the decent thing to do would be to give Herrick the letters.

That Murdock, having reached a decision, then hedged his bet was due to experience that had taught him it was often wise to have a trump card he could use when his judgment was wrong. And so, not knowing what would eventually happen to the letters, he knew he should take the precaution of photographing one or two of the notes, not here where someone might ask questions, but at his apartment where he could work in private.

With the letters in his pocket he snapped off the light and went out to speak to Terry, asking him to print the two negatives for him.

"Sure." Terry put aside his crossword puzzle. "What'll I do with the prints?"

"Stick them under the blotting pad on my desk and let the negatives dry. The boy can file them tomorrow."

One of the first things Kent Murdock had done when he moved into his second-floor apartment several years earlier was to make a deal with the landlord so that he could fix up a darkroom. By putting up a partition in the kitchen, he had sealed off what had originally been a dinette, put in a door, installed a special shade for the window, and added the necessary plumbing to give him a compact but self-contained unit. He had also rigged up a home-made device for copying photographs and papers and now, at nine twenty, he set up his camera and slipped the top letter from under the ribbon.

For an easel he had a piece of plywood that could be fastened vertically to the wall. Thumbtacks had been stuck along one edge and he used four of them to pin the sheet of stationery flat; then, using two more, he stuck the envelope above the sheet so that the name, address, and postmark would be visible. He switched on his lights, adjusted the focus, and clicked the shutter. He repeated the procedure with the second letter, replaced both under the ribbon, put the packet into a drawer. He had disassembled his easel and camera-support and was about to remove the filmholder when the buzzer sounded.

He scowled absently as the sound was repeated, because he did not want company. He also knew that his lights were visible from the street and that it would do no good to pretend he was not at home. And so, reluctantly, he stepped into the kitchen, swinging the darkroom door behind him. He crossed the living room as the buzzer sounded again more insistently.

He said: "Okay, okay," none too pleasantly and turned the knob. He opened the door, stepping back as he did so. The two men who had been waiting in the hall moved quickly across the threshold as a unit, giving him no choice but to retreat still more. By the time he got his balance they were inside.

The manner of entrance and the arrogance displayed stirred Murdock's anger quickly. Knowing only that they were strangers, he was instantly reminded of Felix and Nate, not from any facial similarity but from the knowledge that they presented a physical threat based on muscle and intimidation.

Both were hard-eyed and dark-complected. Both wore blue suits that were snug across the hips; both were bareheaded, but here the similarity ended. For the big man—he was not much taller than Murdock but considerably heavier—bore the marks of his trade: a twisted nose, scarred brows, and lips that had been flattened out of shape. The second, husky but not tall, had a smooth, pointed face, a straight nose, and an underslung jaw that was blue-shadowed and angular.

"What the hell do you want?" Murdock said.

"You're Murdock, aren't you?" The shorter man reached behind him to close the door. The other hand was thrust deep in his jacket pocket, the outline of the fabric suggesting a gun. "You're the photographer?"

"What about it?"

The big man had no gun. His gnarled hands hung halfway to his knees and he began to move laterally round Murdock, his little eyes busy. When he spoke his voice was curiously high pitched for one so large.

"We come for a picture," he said. "Get it up and we'll blow."

"You'll blow anyway."

Murdock looked from one to the other, his dark gaze morose. He did not know which picture they referred to nor, at the moment, did he care. The resentment had built to the point where he was not thinking logically or considering the odds, and what he did then was not very smart.

He had turned as he spoke and two long strides took him to the telephone. He snatched it up, ignoring the big man and punching his finger at the dial. His finger had just started to move when the instrument was snatched from his grasp. Then, as he cocked his left, a hamlike fist clubbed him on the side of the head and he fell over, bouncing on one shoulder and twisting to his knee, not hurt but a little stunned by the force of the blow. His first reaction was instinctive and the desire to attack was strong. His hands came to the floor and his muscles tensed, like a sprinter awaiting the starter's gun. He had his eyes fixed on the big man's belly when the other man spoke.

"Don't try it."

The harsh warning was sufficient to spoil the attempt and start him thinking, and as he watched the big man replace the telephone he began to understand that new tactics were needed. Before he could come to his feet he saw that the second man had pulled out a short-barreled revolver.

"Don't be a chump," he said. "Harry could take you with one hand."

"Maybe," Murdock said, still burning. "Why don't you leave us alone and see." He rose and dusted off his knee.

"What're you waving the gun for if Harry's so good?"

"Because we got a job to do and we get paid to make sure."

"You want a picture," Murdock said. "If you don't get it you start blasting, is that the way it works?"

"Not exactly. But a slug in the knee would put you down long enough for us to take this place apart." He glanced at his companion. "Which is what we may have to do, Harry."

"Why don't you get started then?" Harry said. "If this character wants to slug it out with me we can go a couple of fast rounds while you're looking."

He shifted his weight slightly as he spoke and the flattened lips warped in a grin. His companion glanced at the kitchen door and seemed to be considering the suggestion seriously. At the same time Murdock realized that he could no longer afford the luxury of a healthy anger. His resentment was still nagging him but he remembered the letters he had just photographed and the filmholder that was still in the camera.

"Wait a minute," he said. "What picture are you talking about?"

The man with the gun smiled. "That's better," he said. "What picture? The one you took Saturday night of an accident on the way to the Cape."

"Oh, that," said Murdock, pretending there had been a misunderstanding. "Somebody already swiped those two shots."

"There was another. You took three, remember?"

Murdock sighed softly. So that was it? Someone thought the film he had nearly forgotten was important after all. If young Terry had done his job a print of that negative should be safely tucked away beneath the blotter pad on his desk and it would do no great harm to surrender the film. Yet even as he realized this the stubbornness continued to work on him, and it was characteristic that he refuse to surrender any film under pressure—unless, of course, the pressure got too great.

"I remember," he said, "but I haven't got it now."

"You can get it."

"I doubt it."

"Maybe we can make you try."

"I can make him," Harry said.

"We'll do as we were told," his companion added. "It's like this," he said to Murdock. "You've been a photographer quite a while. We figure you've collected a lot of films and we ain't got time now to go over 'em one by one. So what we do is this: we shake the place down and pick up every lousy one we find and take the bundle with us... Get started, Harry," he said with a sudden snap in his voice.

"I'll watch him."

The suggestion jarred Murdock and he was suddenly more concerned than resentful. Because—just how they should know this there was no way of telling—they were so right about the films. He had hundreds filed away: four by fives, two-and-a-quarter by three-and-a-quarters, thirty-five millimeters. They represented the best of many years of work and he knew that once he lost them he would never get them back.

"You win," he said quickly. "The negative you want is at the paper."

"Yeah?" The shorter man eyed him with suspicion.

"How do we know?"

"I'll get it for you."

"How?"

"I'll call up. I'll have someone bring it over."

He turned again to the telephone, still worried, wanting them to accept the suggestion, willing to compromise this time just so long as they left his collection alone.

"Hold it."

He stopped with his hand on die telephone. The gunman came closer.

"Look up the number of the Courier, Harry," he said.

"Let's be sure he don't get cute... Where's the book?"

Murdock gestured toward the directory underneath the telephone stand. He stood still while Harry found the number and began to dial.

"Who does he ask for?" the gunman said.

"Ask for the studio. I'll take it from there."

He heard Harry repeat the words, and the gun was in his back now as he took the telephone and heard Phil Terry's voice.

"Phil—Kent Murdock. You know that film you developed?" he asked, hoping that Terry would not mention the print. "The one of the traffic accident... Well, can you get a boy to bring it to my place?"

"I'll bring it myself," Terry said. "I'm just going off."

"Right away?"

"Sure... Say, someone called in for you a while ago. I told him you were home. Did you get the call?"

"Yeah," said Murdock dryly. "I got it. See you soon."

He replaced the instrument gently and the gun was no longer in his back. He turned.

"Okay?"

"It's a good start," the gunman said. "Let's sit down and relax. Take that chair by the door."

Murdock did as directed. Harry pulled a straight-backed chair near him, and his companion eased down on the divan, the gun dangling between his legs. They sat that way in complete silence for perhaps ten minutes, until Harry cleared his throat.

"How much longer?"

Murdock glanced at his watch. He said: "Any minute now," and not long after that they heard the buzzer.

"Watch it!" The gunman pocketed the gun but kept his hand on it. "No tricks. Get the film and get rid of him."

Murdock opened the door and Harry moved with him to lean negligently against the wall but no more than an arm's length away.

Terry said: "Hi," and took a step into the room. He reached into his pocket and brought forth a negative. His glance nicked to Harry, to the man on the davenport. Then he hesitated.

Murdock did not know why, but he saw the youth's eyes narrow and things start to happen behind them. It may have been some inner radar that told Terry there was something wrong with the set-up; it may have been a question about the quality of Murdock's visitors or the look in their eyes. Whatever the reason he took another half step. He grinned, still holding on to the negative.

"You got a drink in the place?" he asked.

Under other circumstances Murdock would have been delighted with the young photographer's reaction. In some way of his own he had smelled trouble and now, without knowing the nature of that trouble, he wanted a piece of it. The request for a drink was simply an opening gambit and he was leaving the strategy to Murdock, and Murdock's veto came at once.

Thinking of his films and equipment, and the gun that Terry did not know about, he refused to take a chance. Someone would certainly get hurt and he did not want this to happen to Terry. At that Harry nearly spoiled things.

"No drink, sonny," he said. "Hand it over and blow."

Terry looked at him and his chin moved out a half inch.

"Whose place is this, Fatso?"

"He's right about the drink, Phil," Murdock cut in. "I'm all out. I couldn't even offer my friends a shot." He had the film in his fingers now and he pulled it free as he edged forward to crowd Terry into the doorway.

"You got a raincheck," he added. "And thanks for bringing the negative. See you tomorrow, hunh?"

Terry was in the hall before he knew it. There was a look of puzzlement and disappointment on his cocky young face, but he accepted the decision because it came from his boss.

"Sure," he said as he turned away. "Sure, Kent."

Murdock shut the door and let his breath out slowly. He walked over to the divan and presented the negative as the gunman rose, an odd smile on his dark face.

"That's a smart kid," he said. "Almost too smart. He could've got himself hurt if you hadn't handled him." He held the negative up to the light, squinted at it. "Yeah," he said. "This should be it... Okay, Harry."

He walked over to the door as Harry opened it. "This way is better, ain't it, Murdock?"

"Better than what?"

"Better than havin' us rip the joint apart... See you around."

"Alone, I hope," Murdock said.

He let them close the door, then locked it before he started for the kitchen and darkroom. His thoughts were an odd mixture of relief and frustration as he

automatically took the cover off his developing tank and
snapped off the light. His fingers removed the films from
the holder and put them in the tank. He covered it,
turned on the safelight, set the automatic timer. When it
buzzed, he gave the films a quick wash, transferred them
to the hypo, and stepped into the kitchen to fix a drink.

He stood quite a while sipping his bourbon-and-
water, ankles crossed and his buttocks propped against
the sink. His dark hair was tousled now, the dark eyes
fixed and sightless. The weariness was beginning to show
in his angular face, and in his mind there was only
confusion.

When he finally realized this he took his glass into
the darkroom and put his negatives to wash while he
cleaned up the sink and covered his trays.

Because the packet of letters still bothered him, he
took it to the bedroom and tucked it underneath some
sweaters and golf shirts in the bottom drawer of the
chest. He undressed slowly and went naked into the
bathroom to wash and brush his teeth. When he had
donned pajamas he took his glass back to the kitchen,
made a partial refill, stepped into the darkroom, and
attached clips to the two negatives which he then hung on
a length of wire strung over the small radiator under the
window.

In the morning he would put those negatives in an
envelope and hide them somewhere. He still did not know
what he ought to do about the letters and he was tired
thinking about them. What he wanted now was sleep and
so he started through the apartment to turn out the
lights, glass in hand until he drained it and opened the
bedroom window.

CHAPTER 10

THE FIRST HOUR in the morning was usually a busy one at the studio and Monday was no exception. The assignment book had to be checked with the day city editor, men had to be sent forth in the company radio cars, the business office had to be consulted so that certain pictures could be taken to keep the advertisers happy. When things quieted down there was only Bailey in the anteroom and a veteran named Walt Carey, who was in the printing room finishing up on company time some free-lance job that promised a few extra dollars of liquor money, an essential to Carey's way of life. The radio was quiet. The monitor balanced on top of it—a duplicate of the one in the city room—showed three of the cars were in use, and now Murdock reached for the print under the blotter pad and leaned back to examine it.

He had made sure Terry had put it there when he first came in. He knew that this was the first shot he had taken of the accident, but even as he gave it his attention he could see no reason why it should be important to anyone.

The three or four spectators around the battered car on the road were intent on the wreck and their faces were not revealed. The first car in line behind the accident was clearly indicated but the windshield obscured the driver. The only details visible were the radiator grill, which identified the make, and the front license number.

In itself this was no clue, but as Murdock's brain began to work on the thought he remembered Sam Terroni and his request and his threat. Terroni was not in this picture. Even if the license number was his it would prove nothing, so why should anyone care?

The silent question was enough to prod Murdock's curiosity and he put the print on the desk. There was a magnifying glass in the drawer and when he used it the five-digit number became legible. On impulse then he reached for the telephone and asked for an outside number. One of Murdock's many acquaintances worked for the Motor Vehicle Bureau and when he had his connection he asked for the man and identified himself. They said hello and each asked the other how he was. With such amenities out of the way, Murdock stated his request and repeated the number. He lit a cigarette while he waited, and a minute later he had the information.

"Carl Darrow," the man said. "You want the address?"

Murdock said no, voiced his appreciation, and hung up.

For several minutes then he drew absently on the cigarette and let his mind experiment. Out of this came several conflicting thoughts.

He again told himself that he was not interested in solving a murder and had no intention of doing any private snooping. On the other hand the reason for his callers last night was quite clear, and he understood the necessity for that call. With this photograph in police hands, Carl Darrow no longer had an alibi for the murder of the woman he had been running around with.

The scene of that accident was twenty-five minutes or less from the motel where the woman had been killed. The time was about eight fifty, a fact the state police could verify. This meant that Darrow could have left that motel as late as eight thirty. It meant he could have called on his lawyer here in the city as stated at ten o'clock, but the call he said he had made to the lawyer at nine could have come only from some roadside public telephone. All this made the photograph vital to Darrow, and possibly just as vital to the police. In this instance Murdock knew what his decision was going to be. As if to remind him, his telephone rang and the familiar voice of Lieutenant Bacon came to him.

"I hear," said the lieutenant in his dry laconic tones, "that you fell over another body Saturday night."

"And I hear you're going to be handling the investigation at this end."

"Who said so?"

"Various spies and informers."

Bacon grunted as a signal of reluctant assent. "I've talked to the chief down at Bayview," he said. "Sergeant Keogh's out pounding on doors with a state police lieutenant named Carlin. I've read a copy of a rough transcript. Now I'd like to talk to you."

"This is a switch," Murdock said. "Usually I can't even buy information from you."

"You still can't," Bacon said. "But in this case you're a witness and I can call the shots... You knew the woman, didn't you?"

"Not well."

"How well?"

"She used to work in the business office before she got married. I knew her husband but she was in New York until sometime last spring. I saw her maybe three times since then."

"Okay. When do you want to come down? I'll be out for a while but—"

"Maybe around noon," Murdock said.

He glanced at his watch as he hung up, knowing now that he wanted to see Carl Darrow and wondering how long the session with the police would last at Bayview.

Darrow had been told to be at the station at nine. Murdock did not think he would be detained for long, but when he realized it was still too early to call on Darrow, he went upstairs to talk to the Sunday editor about a picture layout. When he came back a case of whisky was sitting smack in the middle of the anteroom floor.

Bailey, whose doctor had told him he shouldn't drink, was examining some prints, but Walt Carey, who had worn a cap as long as anyone could remember, had pushed it back and was eying the box longingly.

"Scotch," he said reverently. "Twelve years old."

"Whose is it?" Murdock asked.

"Yours."

"Mine?" Murdock circled the case, seeing the envelope tucked in a crack but not touching it. "Where did it come from?"

"This guy walks in with the thing on his shoulder," Carey said, "and says does Murdock work here and I say yes, so he dumps it on the floor and walks out." He straightened and cocked an eye at Murdock. "Some customers you work for. I should have a couple like that." Murdock opened the envelope which contained a single sheet. The penciled message read:

Thanks for the favor.

Appreciate your help... Sam.

Murdock said: "Sam," half to himself, and now the answer came to him. Sam Terroni had played it straight. He had had nothing to do with Lucille Dunn or the theft of the filmholder. He had assumed his threat had carried weight and he was paying off for what he thought had been a favor.

Murdock crumpled the note and envelope as he went to his desk. He looked up Sam Terroni's residence in the directory and dialed the number. The woman who answered gave him another number to call and when he did so he had to wait while someone went in search of Terroni. When he finally had his man his tone was curt and succinct.

"Look, Sam," he said. "I had nothing to do with keeping those pictures out of the paper. I didn't do any favor and I don't want the whisky."

"You listen," Sam said. "I don't know who did me the favor, but you're the guy I talked to. To me it was a favor and for favors I pay off. If you don't want the whisky, toss it out the window."

The telephone clicked dead before Murdock could reply, and when he stood up he had the frustrated and childish feeling that he had somehow been corrupted in spite of himself. He ripped open the case. He glanced at the twelve bottles and knew he could not throw them away just as he knew he would gag if he took a single swallow. Then, an idea coming to him, he counted off the fourteen men who worked for him and found one besides Bailey who didn't drink, a fellow named Wilson who had tried whisky too often and found it an impossible tonic.

A cabinet partition had been erected behind Murdock's office. About desk-high from the floor a broad composition shelf had been fashioned to serve as a table on which the various photographers could write captions and make notes, and above this were rows of sizable pigeonholes.

Each man had his name on one of these, and while the uses were many and varied, the chief function of each box was to provide a repository for mail, messages, and such personal items as struck the fancy.

Now Murdock dragged the case over to the cabinet and began to distribute the whisky. He allocated one bottle to each of the drinkers and as he worked Carey got the idea and spoke up.

"How about me?" he asked anxiously.

"You'll get one," Murdock said. "But it stays in the box until you're through for the day."

"Okay," said Carey. "Sure. But let me hold it for a minute first, will you?"

Murdock gave him the bottle and Carey made a show of cuddling it until Murdock snatched it back, grinning now and his ill-humor forgotten as he rammed the bottle into Carey's box.

Carl Darrow had offices on the fifth floor of a Federal Street building. Murdock had never been there and was not sure just what to expect as he entered an outer room containing two desks, some business machines with stands, a green-metal filing cabinet, and a water cooler.

On the left a door led to some inner room, and he moved to the desk nearest this to make his request.

"I'm not sure," the bespectacled girl said. "Mr. Darrow just came in a few minutes ago. Is he expecting you?"

"Just tell him Kent Murdock is here."

"Well—I'll see."

She stood and opened the door. Beyond, Murdock could see a paneled room, a settee along one wall, the edge of a desk over which the girl now leaned. When she came back a minute later she stood in the doorway and nodded. When Murdock entered he saw that a much prettier girl sat at an executive-type desk near the center of the room.

There were two telephones and an inter-office communicator on the desk, a closed door directly in back of it. Beside the door was a chair, now occupied by a dark-haired man in a neat blue suit. He was young, muscular-looking but not bulky, and until Murdock entered, he apparently had been reading the newspaper. He still held it, but his eyes were visible above the top and the object of their interest was no longer the news columns but Murdock. They picked him up as the girl told him he could go into the next office, and Murdock had the feeling that he was being measured, weighed, assessed as to possible intent, and searched for a concealed weapon all at the same time. Darrow's office was similar to the outer one except that the desk was bigger and the pile on the pale-green rug thicker. There was a leather divan, two leather chairs, and when Darrow felt like swiveling his own chair the two windows would give him a glimpse of the harbor. Now he sat with his elbows on the desk, in shirtsleeves, fingers locked, and his tanned, boxlike face impassive.

"I'm busy this morning, Murdock," he said. "I can give you five minutes."

"That should be enough." Murdock sat in one of the leather chairs. "How's Harry this morning?"

"Harry who?"

"He didn't give me his last name but you know who I mean. The big slob that came to my place last night."

He went on to explain what had happened and there was no interruption as Darrow leaned back and put his hands on the arms of the chair. They were strong-looking hands, the fine black hair on the backs disappearing under French cuffs which held square gold links. Murdock noticed the pattern of overlapping squares as he talked. They made him think of swastikas with a small blue stone in the center. He also noted the platinum-and-star-ruby ring on the little finger.

"It was a good idea," he said; "threatening to clean out my negatives unless I produced a particular one. But I doubt if those two were smart enough to figure it. I think the job was fingered and you made one mistake."

"Why me? I've been legitimate for a long time. I haven't fooled around with muscles for years."

"What do you call that lad outside?"

Darrow moved one thick brow, and a glint of something that might have been amusement touched his eyes.

"Leslie's my driver."

"Complete with gun?"

"I've made quite a pile, Murdock. There are some oldtimers around that would like to clip me if they got the chance, and like I say: personally I don't like muscle. Leslie is a legitimate business deduction... But assuming I did finger the job, what was the mistake?"

"It just happened that a print of that negative had been made. It was in my desk at the office. I gave it a look this morning, and since you don't know anything about it, let me tell you what that picture was."

Murdock took his time and his explanation of the accident and the pictures he had taken was concise; so was the deduction he then made.

"That photograph knocks the alibi you produced down at Bayview right out the window."

"Not quite," Darrow said. "It puts my car on the road, but it doesn't put me in it."

"It makes you think again though, doesn't it?"

Darrow considered the question. He swiveled his chair to face Murdock; then reached for a mahogany humidor and removed a cigar. He took out a gold cutter before he remembered his manners.

"Oh." He pushed the humidor toward the end of the desk. "Cigar?"

Murdock shook his head, feeling a certain admiration for the man's aplomb and watching him clip the end and roll the cigar gently between his hps. When he had a light, Darrow puffed a moment and then said:

"What's bugging you, Murdock? Are you playing cop now? Is there a reward out you'd like a piece of?" Murdock eyed the other directly and smiled, not enthusiastically but enough to let Darrow know the needle wasn't bothering him.

"I don't like people interfering with my work—which is taking pictures. I don't like being pushed around."

"Who does?" Darrow shrugged and examined the end of his cigar. "What did you do with the picture?"

Murdock hesitated. The photograph had been rolled up and now rested in his inside pocket, but since a small lie seemed in order he said:

"I sent it down to Lieutenant Bacon by messenger. I'm seeing him later and you'll probably be hearing from him."

He rose and straightened his jacket. "The thing that gets me is how you stayed tangled up with a woman like Hazel Franklin for so long. You've got money, good looks. You know your way around and"—he made a small bow—"if I may say so, you have a very attractive wife."

If Darrow took offense he did not show it. He continued to take small puffs on his cigar and turned his chair still more so that his gaze moved to one of the windows. When he finally spoke the words seemed directed more at himself than at Murdock.

"I used to wonder myself. I still don't know what it was that Hazel had. Sure she was good-looking, but no knockout. Sexy? In a way, but it was something more, something you knew wasn't very good and yet you kept trying to find out what it was. I paid six fifty for a mink stole—she was a selfish, greedy dame and you knew that too—and twenty-five for a diamond wrist watch that somebody stole—"

He stopped abruptly, as though realizing the monologue was too personal to be voiced before a witness. He turned his chair to face Murdock and his tone was again matterof-fact and indifferent.

"I'll be glad to talk to Bacon," he said. "I'll even give him some advice: Find the guy who stole that watch and the two rings and he'll have his killer... Well, thanks for the warning, Murdock." He grunted softly as he gave his attention to the papers on his desk. "I'll do the same for you some time."

Murdock accepted his dismissal. When he opened the door and glanced back, Darrow was still busy.

CHAPTER 11

IT WAS twelve thirty when Kent Murdock walked into a bare and uninviting room which was furnished with several battered desks and chairs to match. Two detectives were busy at typewriters banging out reports and a third, who had been reading a newspaper, glanced up, recognized Murdock, and gave him a twisted nod that was silent permission to enter the closed door beyond.

As an office, Lieutenant Bacon's inner sanctum was no more prepossessing than Murdock's, even though it was somewhat larger. There was room for two extra chairs, but there was only one window, and Bacon was contemplating the view of the brick wall opposite when Murdock came in. Turning only his head in that first moment, Bacon scowled at his visitor, not with animosity but simply to keep in practice. Murdock ignored the scowl and sat down. In a voice that was mockingly subservient, he said:

"I'm here, sir... You wanted to see me?"

Bacon snorted his disapproval but he got his feet on the floor and hunched his long body over the desk, a bean pole of a man with graying hair and alert gray eyes that seldom smiled, not because he had no sense of humor but because he had learned to keep a suspicious mind and preferred to remain outwardly neutral when possible.

"Start at the beginning," he directed. "Everything."

"You've heard it if you talked to Chief Nickerson."

"I got time."

Murdock complied, editing as he went along but giving the facts that dealt with his finding of Hazel Franklin's body. When he finished he said:

"What've you found out this morning at this end?"

"A few little things."

"Like what?"

"They're not for publication."

"I'll make a deal."

"No deal."

"I might have a lead for you."

Bacon's eyes opened a little but he was still suspicious. Murdock understood the reaction because he had known Bacon a long time and, within limits, could almost sense how his mind would work. By practice and training, Bacon played by the book, but there were ways of getting his guard down. In this case the feeling of respect was mutual, and Murdock had an idea that if he opened up Bacon would, in the end, speak of the few little things he had heretofore refused to discuss. Now, taking the rolled photograph from his pocket, he straightened it deliberately.

He examined it while he waited for Bacon's outburst. Presently it came.

"Come on, damn it!" he snapped. "What's the lead?" He held his hand out and Murdock passed over the photograph, watching the scowl deepen until Bacon glanced up. "What is it? What kind of a lead is this?"

"It'll take a while."

"I told you I had time."

Murdock crossed his knees and began to talk. He started with the accident and the three photographs he had taken. He mentioned Sam Terroni and Lucille Dunn; he spoke of his discovery that the two films she had taken had been developed and destroyed at the Blue Heron, and he ended up by describing the two men who had crashed his apartment the night before.

Bacon had some difficulty digesting the story. He listened intently and from time to time he would glance at the photograph he still held, but what had been wrinkles in his brow became deep grooves and his keen gray eyes held a baffled look as Murdock finished.

"Let's start in the middle," he said finally. "This is the picture the blonde didn't get?"

"Right."

"What makes it important?"

"The license number."

"Oh?" He tipped his head. "You check it yet?"

"Carl Darrow."

"Ahh—" He dropped the photograph on the desk and thought a bit longer. "You took it around ten of nine. Darrow said he was in town at nine. This sort of proves he wasn't. So what's your theory?"

"I haven't got one," Murdock said.

"Nuts!" Bacon made the word sound like a curse. "You've always got a theory. I've never seen such a guy for theories. Sometimes you're even right."

Murdock grinned at him and reached for a cigarette. "I can make some guesses—but so can you."

"Let's hear yours."

"Someone drove Hazel Franklin to the Pine Grove Motel, and she registered with a phony license number. It could have been Darrow—he'd been running around with her—but it doesn't have to be. Maybe he killed her and maybe not, but it looks as if he knew she was dead—and found out about it not long after it happened."

"Why?"

Murdock lit the cigarette and sucked in a mouthful of smoke. His dark eyes were serious now because he was trying hard to put together a logical sequence of the facts he knew.

"Just assume that much," he said. "If you won't buy that the theory is a bust and I'm wasting my breath."

"I don't know why you think so, but go ahead."

"Darrow knew. If so he also knew he would be an immediate suspect because of his association with the woman. He needed an alibi in a hurry, and my guess is that he drove to the Blue Heron and picked up Lucille Dunn, turned around, and high-tailed it for Boston. What he told the girl and how much it cost him we don't know, but his idea was probably to have dinner here in town with her and then drive back to the Blue Heron. He would have been seen having dinner with her at, say, a quarter of ten, but she could say she had been with him since eight o'clock."

"The accident loused up the plan, is that your idea?"

"Yes. I don't believe that story about the girl's boyfriend kicking her out. If I'm right about that, how else could she be out there in the country at that time? . . . So I say she was with Darrow. He saw me take the pictures and he was afraid—and he was right—that I might have caught his license number. He had to have that picture because he couldn't take the risk that it might be published."

He took another drag on his cigarette and said: "He had a tough choice. He knew he would be suspected and he also knew that if the police ever saw that picture they could place him close to the scene of the murder at an awkward time. To lose the girl would mean he'd have to cook up a different alibi, but he decided to take that chance. I think he gave her the story of the boyfriend and told her what to do."

"She gave you the con and the big smile," said Bacon, "and you bit. She was a good-looking number, hunh?"

"Very."

"Then it was a cinch you'd buy the story."

"So would you," Murdock said defensively.

"Maybe." Bacon pushed his hps out and sucked them back. "If I accept that I guess I have to accept the business of her taking your car long enough to get the filmholder. She got a cab to the Blue Heron, talked her photographer friend into developing the film to make sure she had the accident pictures. When Darrow finally showed up just before midnight she gave him the word. But she missed one shot because you had that filmholder in your pocket."

"Umm," he said. "Yeah. And if I go along that far I can see why Darrow would send those two hoods to your place. He was still trying... But he did see his lawyer at ten. We've checked that. The lawyer says Darrow phoned at nine—"

"He could have done that as soon as traffic started moving after the accident," Murdock said. "With dial phones there's no way of telling where a call comes from."

Bacon opened a drawer and brought forth a long, slim cigar that looked singularly unimpressive. He had been smoking them ever since Murdock knew him. Little Wonder Panatelas was the trade name, and Bacon bought them by the box at five cents apiece. When he had manicured one end with the same loving care he would have lavished on a Corona-Corona, he wet the tip, rolling it gently between his hps.

"Yeah," he said, sounding much more amiable. "Darrow'll have fun explaining this." He tapped the photo graph and then picked up a pencil. "You say this blonde's name is Lucille Dunn? Any idea where I could find her?"

Murdock ground out his cigarette. "You could try the Hotel Lynn."

Bacon's eyes opened a trifle. "You been around there already?" He watched Murdock shake his head, then said:

"You know a lot of things this morning."

"I doubt if you'll do much good there," Murdock said.

"She'll deny I picked her up or that she took the filmholder—"

"Sure, sure," Bacon cut in. "Your word against hers, but if she's as cute as you say she is I'd like to have a look myself."

"What about the missing jewelry?"

"It's still missing."

"Have you been over Mrs. Franklin's apartment?"

"With a comb. Nothing there that helps."

"Any relatives?"

"A brother. We're trying to raise him in New York."

"What about her bank account?"

"We checked that too."

Bacon lit his cigar expertly and blew out the match. He took a few experimental but tidy puffs and began to rock gently in his chair. With a sidewise glance he said:

"Do you know a guy named George Emerly?"

"Yes."

"Paul Herrick?"

"Yep."

"Any connection between the two?"

"Not that I know of. Emerly's a writer and Herrick's a musician. Why?"

"It looks like this dame had a racket. She's been depositing two hundred and twenty-five bucks a week for several months. Before that there was an entry of twenty-five hundred. We wondered why, so we got the bank to give us a look at the checks she deposited. They photograph 'em these days—"

"With a Recordak."

"Is that what they call those machines? Well, anyway, Emerly and Herrick are the lads that have been getting up the dough—Herrick for an even hundred and Emerly for a hundred and a quarter. According to this"— he tapped some typescript on his desk—"she did some typing for Emerly. For a hundred-and-a-quarter she must've been putting in a lot of overtime."

Murdock had the answer for this as he recalled Emerly's story and his concern. The details given him on the ride back to Bayview Saturday night were still clear, but he was not sure whether he should tell Bacon now or let Emerly do it personally. To temporize he said:

"Have you asked them about it?"

"No, but I'm going to. How well do you know Herrick?"

"Not too well."

"Emerly?"

"For years. He used to work on the Courier."

"Then let's go see him now. You can introduce me."

He stood up and reached for his hat, a gray felt that had been re-blocked but still looked neat. He put it on the center of his head and then, his gaze meeting Murdock's directly, he digressed.

"There's one other bit—not for publication. Mrs. Darrow flew up from Florida on Saturday. She got in town at five o'clock, which would give her plenty of time to get to that motel by eight. That is, if she had any ideas and the right sort of information. I haven't talked to her yet but I will."

He opened the door. "Makes you wonder, hunh? That Franklin woman wasn't too husky, was she? And when you get a stocking around a neck like that it wouldn't take too much muscle would it... Have you ever seen this Mrs. Darrow? How's she built?"

"Very nicely," Murdock said, "if you like your women tall and well proportioned."

CHAPTER 12

GEORGE EMERLY was clad in slacks, slippers, and an old sweater when he opened the door of his apartment, which was on the third floor of a modest building in the Fenway district. He seemed a bit surprised to see Murdock but smiled quickly as he said hello. He stood aside so they could enter, giving Bacon no more than a brief glance until Murdock introduced him.

"Come in," he said. "I've been expecting someone from your office, Lieutenant."

Bacon, who had made a quick inspection of Emerly, did the same thing to the living room before he replied.

"Is that so?" His glance came back and his tone was flat, noncommittal and, to one who did not know him, quite possibly disconcerting. "Why?"

"Well—I mean—" Emerly made embarrassed noises in his throat. "After all, I was questioned in Bayview. I didn't think that would be the end of it... Unless, of course, you've already solved the case."

"We haven't," Bacon said. "Let's sit down and discuss it, Mr. Emerly."

"Fine. Shall we go in here?"

He led the way across the living room, which comfortably furnished but not elaborate. The davenport and the two upholstered chairs looked worn but not shabby, there were a half dozen black-and-white prints on the walls, and the built-in bookcase that stood between the two windows was full.

Murdock, who had been here before, knew that there were two bedrooms, one of which had been converted into a study, and Emerly led them to the doorway and waved them inside. Bacon took the leather chair in the corner and put his hat on one bony knee. Murdock sat down on the studio couch, and Emerly went round behind a desk that was cluttered with typescript, reference books, and ash trays. A water glass held eight or ten sharpened pencils, and a typewriter, a piece of copy still in it, stood at one end of a metal stand.

Emerly sat back and clasped his hands behind his neck and waited for the inquisition to begin. Bacon obliged him.

"How long has Mrs. Franklin been working for you, Mr. Emerly?"

"Ever since she came here from New York in the spring."

"About that time you gave her a substantial sum of money."

"Twenty-five hundred dollars."

"You've been paying her a hundred and a quarter a week ever since. She must have done a lot of work to earn that kind of pay."

"She got twenty-five for the copying she did. The other hundred was for something else." Emerly's bespectacled eyes touched Murdock and came back. "I told Kent about it when we rode down to Bayview Saturday night—Sunday morning, really. I guess he didn't tell you."

Bacon gave Murdock a scathing glance and there was an undertone of sarcasm in his reply. "Murdock doesn't always confide in me."

"I thought it would be simpler if you got the story direct," Murdock said. "That's why we're here, isn't it?"

"The whole thing is sort of complicated," Emerly said.

"Try it on me for size," Bacon said. "Maybe I can follow it."

"Well"—Emerly sighed—"it goes back to a guy named Ted Franklin who used to be a reporter on the Courier."

"This was Mrs. Franklin's husband?"

Emerly said yes and then he was repeating the details he had given Murdock Saturday night. He spoke with care and did his best to be explicit, as though aware that Bacon could not be expected to know the vagaries of the writing business.

Because he knew what was coming, Murdock did not try to follow the account; instead his mind went back to the letters signed Paul. They were still in the bottom drawer of the bedroom chest, and the two negatives he had made were in an envelope secreted between the box spring and mattress on his bed. What made them seem even more important now was the information Bacon had passed along: that Paul Herrick had been paying Hazel Franklin a hundred dollars a week for a considerable period.

Herrick had admitted to seeing Hazel in New York. The phrasing of the letter Murdock had scanned suggested that this had been a passionate affair. Now Herrick was in love again. He intended to marry a girl whose father could assure his musical future. In the hands of a woman like Hazel those letters were a definite threat to that future, and it seemed reasonable to assume that it was to hold off this threat that Herrick had been paying tribute. The weekly payment would be considerable to a man who had never made the musical big time, and everyone who knew Hazel testified to her greediness. Suppose then that she had made new demands that Herrick could not, or would not, fulfill.

Based on such assumptions, the motive for murder was there. In addition Murdock had seen a man who looked like Herrick drive a car out of the Pine Grove Motel some time around nine thirty the night of the murder. Testimony given at Bayview said that Herrick had been eating dinner from seven thirty until some time after eight thirty, except for a brief period when he had answered a telephone call. From the motel?

To make an appointment with Hazel? Why else would he have driven to the motel later? There could be other reasons, but it seemed likely that Herrick knew Hazel Franklin was staying there.

The thought stuck there as he saw Bacon move to the desk and take a sheet from a small pad. Reluctantly he brought his mind into focus, understanding that Emerly's explanation was over and that Bacon wanted details.

"Let's do a little arithmetic." Bacon found a pencil and sat down again. "I got the general idea okay but I want to break it down... Now you sold the first story based on Franklin's old idea for twelve hundred and fifty bucks, right? Have you got the story there?"

Emerly swiveled his chair and leaned over to open the bottom drawer of a multiple-decked filing cabinet. He flipped his fingers across the tops of the manuscripts resting there.

"These are the Franklin stories—originals and carbons —I haven't used. How many I might have used in the future under the contract Hazel and I signed I haven't any idea." He opened the next drawer and took out a manuscript.

"This is a Franklin story I did use. The first one, as a matter of fact. The two copies he left behind, the rough draft I made of it, and a carbon of my final version." He touched a slip of paper that had been clipped to the title page. "This is what happened to it. Who bought it and for how much."

He twisted his lanky body to see if Bacon was following him and then opened the drawer above. It was full of manuscript, but unlike that in the other drawers the pages were of yellow copy-paper instead of white.

"These are all my own stories. There's a record on each one because not all of them sold. This one here is the fiction piece I did after I had rewritten a couple of Franklin's, the one I sold to TV and the movies." He indicated another script. "This is another in the same field that I couldn't peddle." He brought forth a bulkier script. "This is the original of my book which will be out shortly. The carbon of the final draft is in the top drawer."

Bacon handed back the manuscript he had been examining. "All right," he said, "let's get back to the bookkeeping. You got twelve fifty for this. How much for the next?"

"Fifteen hundred."

"The next?"

"Fifteen hundred plus fifteen more for an hour TV show."

"The next?"

"Chronologically the next was my own. So was the one after that, but it didn't sell. The next Franklin job went for two thousand plus two thousand. I've started on another one but it isn't finished."

Bacon, who had been making notes, said: "The Franklin stuff adds up to ninety-seven fifty... She recognized her husband's stuff and came up here and threatened you?"

"That's right."

"You thought Franklin had been divorced, but he hadn't, and you worked out a deal where she was to get half of the dough you'd collected. That would be half of ninety-seven fifty."

"Less commission. I've got an agent."

"How much is that?"

"Ten per cent. Nine seventy-five."

Bacon made another note of subtraction. "That leaves eighty-seven seventy-five." He took out a small notebook and consulted it. "You paid her twenty-five hundred originally and a hundred a week for eighteen weeks. That's forty-three hundred. In other words, you lacked only eighty-seven bucks of being even."

Emerly shut the file drawers and turned back t;o the desk. "That's right."

"Why didn't you pay her off in the first place?"

Emerly grinned crookedly and ran his fingers through the graying sandy hair.

"I didn't have the cash at the time. Hell, Lieutenant, I had to pay taxes on that money and I'd spent most of it. I could have cleaned it up out of advances on the book, but by that time she liked the hundred-a-week idea." Bacon put his hat on and replaced his automatic pencil. He folded his notes and pocketed the slip.

"This last story," he said, "the one that isn't finished— would that have been a fifty-fifty deal or under the contract?"

"Contract," Emerly said. "That's why I made it."

"Have you got a copy?"

"Certainly."

Emerly opened a drawer and offered a carbon of the one-page agreement Murdock had seen in Hazel Franklin's apartment Saturday night. He watched Bacon's eyes travel back and forth and finally fix on Emerly.

"This is dated a month ago."

"Sure." Emerly chuckled softly. "It took that long before she'd buy the twenty-five per cent deal. When she saw it was that or nothing, she signed." He hesitated, brow furrowing. "I wonder what I do now."

"About what?" Bacon asked.

"Who do I pay in case I want to use any more of Franklin's stories? I think she had a brother—"

"In New York. We're trying to get in touch with him. If he inherits—a lawyer'll know about that—maybe you can make a new deal with him. Or maybe the original contract holds. I don't know enough about law to say."

He thought a moment and said: "There's one thing more. You used to see her nearly every day. You knew she had been running around with Carl Darrow. What did she say about him? How do you think they got along?"

"All right, I guess," Emerly said. "She came in one day with a mink stole and modeled it for me. I asked her where she got it and she said her boyfriend gave it to her. When I asked if she meant Darrow she just grinned and got mysterious... Then a while after that she showed me a platinum-and-diamond wrist watch. She said something about knowing how to pick her boyfriends."

"She didn't actually mention Darrow?"

"No."

"What about Paul Herrick?"

"I don't know that she ever mentioned him."

"You didn't know she'd been collecting a hundred a week from him too?"

"No, I didn't. Why should he—"

"We're not sure yet." Bacon rose and adjusted his hat to make sure it was placed dead center on his graying head.

"Thanks for the co-operation, Mr. Emerly," he said. "We may want you to put all of this on paper so the D.A. can understand the facts. I'll let you know."

"I'll be glad to."

Emerly stood and touched Murdock's arm as Bacon left the room. He spoke softly as they moved toward the door. "Thanks for the advice you gave me Saturday night, and thanks for coming along. It made things a hell of a lot easier." .

Murdock said to forget it. He said it was Bacon's idea.

Murdock lunched late that day, and because he was not very hungry he stopped at a tavern around the corner from the *Courier* to get a hot corned-beef sandwich and a beer. He had managed rather successfully to get his mind off the business of murder, when someone pulled out the chair on the opposite side of his table. Before he could glance up a friendly voice said:

"Hello, Mr. Murdock. All right if I sit down a minute?"

Murdock's eyes widened; then he grinned.

"Hey, Charlie," he said. "What brings you to town? Sit down. Have you had your lunch?"

Charlie Lane seemed different in his city clothes, and Murdock realized this was the first time he had ever seen him in a suit and wearing a tie. He looked very neat but somehow uncomfortable, and his sunburned, wrinkled face seemed even more noticeable against the white background of his shirt.

"I've had my lunch, thanks," he said when he had settled himself. "They told me at your office you might be here."

"Well, how about coffee?"

"Coffee would be fine."

Murdock gave the waiter the order and took another bite of his sandwich. He watched Charlie examine his surroundings. When the eyes remained evasive, he said:

"When'd you get up?"

"This morning. I got me a room for a few days."

"Before you go to Florida?"

"That's what I hope. That's what I wanted to talk to you about."

He leaned back as the waiter deposited the coffee. He spooned sugar and stirred. He kept stirring and seemed intent on the whirlpool he was creating. He was having trouble with his next sentence and when it came he was still looking at his cup.

"A paper like the *Courier* sometimes pays for tips, don't it?"

"What kind of tips, Charlie?"

"Well—you know. Tips that give them information, or a story?"

Murdock's feeling of easy amiability fled instantly with that question. In its place there came the stirring of suspicion that brought an odd sense of shock and concern. It was not just the words but the evasive manner in which they had been spoken, a manner so unlike the Charlie Lane he knew that he sought some other answer.

"Sometimes," he said quietly. "It depends on a lot of things."

Charlie put his spoon aside and took a sip of coffee. His glance was still averted and when he did not speak Murdock prompted him.

"Have you got something you think we can use?"

"I was wondering. That's why I wanted to talk to you."

Murdock put his sandwich down and there was a curious stillness inside him as he leaned forward. "Does it have to do with what happened Saturday night?"

"Yes."

Murdock hesitated again but he could not keep his thoughts still. He remembered the twenty-dollar bills Charlie had on the golf course, just as he recalled the statement by someone in the Bayview police station that there had been twenty dollars in Hazel Franklin's wallet. Yet it had been his impression that there had been several bills in that wallet when he first examined it while looking for some identification.

He could not speak of this to Charlie Lane now because there could be other explanations. Even if Charlie had slipped those few bills into his pocket while waiting for the police, Murdock could understand it. Charlie wanted get-away money. Here was a chance to get some that no one would know about and the dead woman could not miss. But this was a petty thing and unimportant now. . . .

"Look, Charlie," he said. "If it has to do with murder don't you think you ought to go to the police?"

"The police? Hah!" Charlie's gaze leveled then and there was a note of bluster, possibly defensive, in his tone. "Why should I go to them? They never did anything for me but push me around when I was broke. They don't pay for information." He gulped more coffee and put the cup down hard.

"And anyway who says it had anything to do with murder? I don't know who killed that woman. This is just something I saw. Maybe it could be important. Maybe, you understand? So I thought if I told you, it might be a lead you could use. If you followed it up and it was important, and you got a big story out of it, why then you'd get the credit, the paper I mean, and maybe it would be worth paying something for."

It was quite a speech for Charlie, but Murdock knew what he meant. Such knowledge only made him feel worse. He also sensed that with Charlie in his present mood it would be futile to argue.

"How much did you have in mind?" he asked. "Well, I thought if I could get maybe two fifty I'd be set." He pushed the cup aside. "'Course if you ain't interested, forget it. It was just an idea."

"I didn't say I wasn't interested. But I don't have the authority to give you a yes or no right here. I'd have to speak to the managing editor—and I will. But I ought to explain how a thing like this works; at least how it usually works."

He waited for Charlie's eyes to meet his and when he failed he said: "If I get an okay we'd probably give you fifty bucks to listen to your story. Then we'd have to see how important it was to us and whether it was something we could use. If we thought so—and we'd have to be the judge—and we got a story out of it, you'd get your other two hundred. But if we didn't like it, or couldn't use it, we'd drop it and tell you so. You could keep the fifty but that would be it... Where can I reach you later? What's the address of this room?"

He wrote down the street number Charlie gave him. "Is there a phone?"

"Yeah, but it's down on the first floor. I'd better call you, Mr. Murdock."

"Fine. What time do you think?"

Char he considered this. He rubbed his round sunburned nose and pushed back his chair.

"Would nine o'clock be too late for you?"

"No—if that's the best you can do."

Charlie nodded and stood up. "Just one thing. This I told you in confidence because I know you're a square guy. You don't go to the cops with this, do you?"

"Not until after we've talked again." Murdock could have added that if the information helped the murder investigation Charlie would be an important witness whether he liked it or not. Instead he said: "If you go to the police that will be your decision."

"Okay. Maybe I ought to do some more thinking about this but I'll call you at nine anyway. Right?"

Murdock nodded and watched the man walk away.

When he looked down at the remains of his sandwich he was no longer hungry.

CHAPTER 13

WHEN MURDOCK got back to his office and took care of some details that had accumulated during his absence, he did something that had been in the back of his mind on and off all day. Viewed sensibly he had a hard time justifying the impulse that made him look up the number of the Hotel Lynn. It was not, he told himself, because he was interested in the murder. Nor was he ready to admit it was the girl herself who intrigued him. The answer he finally accepted was that he wanted to take her out and get a few drinks into her and persuade her by one means or another to admit that his theory about her was the right one and that she had indeed acted on Carl Darrow's instructions. Yet for all this ratiocination he knew, as he spoke to the desk clerk and asked for her room, that this was a mental fabrication. He wanted to see her because he wanted to find out what she was really like.

"Lucille?" he said when he heard her voice.

"Yes. Who's this?"

"I don't know if you know me by name or not," Murdock said. "But we've met."

"Have we?" The voice was still suspicious. "Where?"

"I'm the guy who got tossed out of your cottage Saturday night, remember?"

"Remember? I'll say I remember," she said crisply.

"Your name is Murdock and you've got an awful nerve calling me after what you did."

"What did I do?"

"You told the police some silly story and a Lieutenant Bacon and another man questioned me for an hour. In fact, they just left."

"How do you know I told them anything?"

"Because they said you did."

"And what did you tell them?"

"I told them I never heard of you. I said I never rode in your car or stole any films and that if you said so you must have been drunk."

"I figured it would come out that way."

"So what do you want now? If you're going to keep giving me that same tired routine the answer is no."

"There'll be no routine. That isn't what I had in mind."

"I'm listening, but not very hard."

"I thought we might have dinner and go out on the town."

"With you?" she said, making the suggestion sound preposterous. "Give me one good reason."

"I'll give you several."

Murdock took a breath and concentrated on the game. He knew that as long as he could keep her talking he was still in business and so he turned on the charm, which, at times, could be considerable. There were also occasions when he was smart enough to sense the soft spots in a woman's armor. It was not always the same spot, but he picked shrewdly this time.

"I talked to Paul Herrick about you Saturday night at the Blue Heron," he said. "He told me you wanted to sing. He said you might have a chance."

"Oh?" Silence. "What else did he say?"

"I can tell you better over a drink. Or maybe a steak or a lobster... I'm really a pretty nice guy," he said. "My manners are good, I'm considerate, and I never get fresh without provocation."

"You won't get any from me," she said, but there was a hint of a smile in her voice now and Murdock pressed his advantage.

"And even if you disliked me I think it would be a mistake to say no just because we had a little trouble Saturday night. That is, if you want to be a singer."

"Oh?" A little curious now. "How do you figure that?"

"I've worked for the *Courier* a long time. I know people. Our entertainment editor, for instance," he said. "And he knows every night spot in town and the owner, the headwaiter, and the orchestra leader. He knows people at the radio and television stations; producers, directors. A smart girl ought to cultivate—"

Her laughter cut him off. "What a salesman!" she said.

"But I'm right."

"I know you're right," she admitted.

"You have to get around and hope for the breaks."

"And you'll introduce me to your editor? Not tonight but maybe sometime. You might even get me an audition."

"It's possible."

Her laughter came again but more softly. When she spoke her words had a different cadence and the hostility was gone.

"I was only kidding about the audition," she said, "but I half believe you. I'm even beginning to think you might be a nice guy. That approach of yours—did you do it off the cuff?—is kind of cute. So if you still want to, I'll buy half of the proposition."

"Which half?"

"The dinner. That on-the-town business is out for tonight."

"Do you know Murphy's? Or do you want something more elegant?"

"Murphy's will be fine."

"Shall I pick you up?"

"I"ll meet you there. How about seven o'clock?"

"Righto... 'Bye."

Murdock hung up, a big grin on his face. He felt, in that instant, like a teen-ager who had just made an important conquest—until he heard a chuckle and glanced round to find Delaney and Klime watching from the doorway.

"Boy!" they said. "Some operator!"

"Beat it," Murdock said, still grinning.

"Sure," they said. "We just wanted to know who to thank for that cookin' whisky that was in our boxes."

"Santa Claus."

"Thanks, Santa," they said.

A call came in on the company radio then and Murdock listened in because he had a photographer in that car. He heard the instructions from the city desk and made a note of them. When the phone rang a minute later he listened to some demand by the business office, and for a while after that he was busy with his job.

It was some time before he had a chance to go upstairs and knock at the managing editor's office. T. A. Wyman told him to come in, tucked the half-smoked cigar in one corner of his month, and listened to Murdock's story about Charlie Lane. When it was over Wyman nodded his approval.

"I'll go along with you," he said. "You never can tell about these guys who think they have information. Sometimes it pays off... You figure it has something to do with the murder?"

"Yes. He claims he doesn't know who did it, but he must know something."

"When you talk to him at nine, try to get him in here. We'll get someone to sit with you. Pay him the fifty bucks and pump him. If it turns out he has something that should go to the police, that's what we'll have to do. Until then let's play along."

Murphy's was noted for good food, if one stuck to the fundamentals and had no interest in fancy dishes and sauces, and the decor was basically pleasant; some chrome, a few mirrors, some red banquettes of simulated leather.

Murdock, arriving at one minute before seven, paced the small foyer opposite the hatcheck counter for ten more minutes before the revolving door ejected Lucille Dunn, and he decided then and there that he was very glad to see her.

Her blonde prettiness was as he remembered, but dressed for the city in a cloth coat and a simple black dress that did nice things for her slenderly rounded body, she was smarter-looking and more sophisticated than he had expected. She smiled when she saw him, and if there were wary glints in her blue eyes he pretended not to notice. They shook hands formally and he told her it was nice of her to come.

"Am I late?"

"Not very," he said, and then he had her by the arm, turriing her toward the doorway and the headwaiter. They settled for a table by the wall and he helped her slip out of her coat. She straightened her shoulders to lift the well defined line of her bosom, touched the back of her feathered hairdo, examined the room with interest, and smiled up at the captain when Murdock asked what she would like to drink.

"Scotch-on-the-rocks," she said, "with a twist of lemon."

"Two," Murdock said.

Sitting shoulder to shoulder as they were, he had to turn to look at her. He had never been this close to her before and he saw that her tanned skin was smooth and unblemished, which made him wonder if she was younger than he had first suspected. Her mouth, with its short upper lip, was neatly outlined in red but not overdone, there was a touch of mascara and shadow around her eyes, and he had an idea that the blondness was basically natural.

As his eyes met hers it surprised him to find that she was inspecting him with some thoroughness, her glance touching his hair, his eyes, his mouth, not boldly but without coyness. Finally she smiled and said:

"Before you give me the usual opening about how did I get in this business—whatever that is—and what is a nice girl like me doing spending her life in night clubs, I'll give you the vital statistics and then we can talk about something else. Okay?"

"You're twenty-four," Murdock said, grinning at her unaffected forthrightness.

"You're a liar. I'm twenty-two."

"And about thirty-seven, twenty-four, thirty-five."

The unexpected statement opened her eyes. "How do you know?"

"I saw you pretty well stripped down once, remember?"

"That's right." She giggled, and an incipient blush touched her cheeks. "You did." She hesitated, as though trying to remember what she had been saying and then continued.

"I'm five, seven and a half in my bare feet. I weigh one hundred and twenty-four pounds. I did not come from a broken home. My father was not a drunkard, there was no actual poverty, and I doubt if I'm any more neurotic than anyone else... How's that for a start?"

She watched the waiter put down the drinks; then lifted her glass. Murdock touched the rim of his to hers and they drank. She rearranged the little paper daily and centered her glass on it before she considered the menu that had been placed before her. Murdock asked if she would like a lobster, because if she did they could order now because it would take a while.

"I'd like a lobster."

"Potatoes?"

"With lobster it doesn't matter much. French-fried will do."

"Salad?"

"Please."

Murdock gave the order and said how about another drink. She asked if he was going to have one and he said he was. Actually he hoped she would drink at least three, and his motive was not entirely honest. He still wanted to get a bit more information about her part in the Saturday night affair and he thought the alcohol might loosen her tongue. But even in this she surprised him.

"In that case," she said, "may I have a shrimp cocktail while you're drinking? I'm hungry."

Murdock laughed because her frankness pleased him.

The captain, who had overheard this, got Murdock's nod of assent, made an additional note on the check, and whisked the menus off the table.

"Now," said the girl, "where was I? Have you heard enough?"

"Not nearly."

She tipped her hand away from the glass and put it back.

"For a dinner like this," she said, 'you're entitled to some information... My name isn't Lucille Dunn, it's Ruth Dumpley."

"What's the matter with Ruth?'"

"It sounds—bovine. Is that the right word?"

"There was a Ruth Etting."

"Ahh—but only one... My father was a mechanic," she said. "Automobiles. He was a partner in a small garage, and while we didn't have many luxuries we had all we needed. As a senior in high school there was a student six-piece band that got about one playing date a week and they used to let me sing—for nothing. The summer after I graduated I did some work with a small professional group that no one ever heard of, but it was enough to make me want to keep trying.

"I was just nineteen when I had a brilliant idea," she said, a note of mild irony in her voice. "I ran away and got married—against my father's wishes. And my father was right. Legally it lasted six months; actually a week finished us. Not because I'm frigid but because we suddenly discovered we had nothing in common but music and it wasn't enough. We simply couldn't stand each other and that was that... I may try it again some day but I have to find out if I can really sing professionally first."

The shrimps came and she attacked them in a neat but businesslike way while Murdock sipped his second drink and thought about the things she had said. This, he decided, was a smart girl, and it surprised him to realize that he liked her very much indeed. He also knew that she would never get drunk unless she wanted to and that the only way he could ever get any information she did not want to give would be because she liked him and felt she could trust him. Now he watched her put her fork aside, lean back, and pat her mouth lightly with the napkin.

"That was good," she said, and smiled. "I really was hungry, wasn't I?" She studied him a moment, the blue eyes serious. "I like working in night clubs," she said, not defensively but like a person stating a fact. "I've worked in a lot of them. I can dance a little. I can do a time step if I have to but if you can be a combination hat-check cigarette girl in the right sort of place you can get more money. Maybe I haven't got much of a voice, but that didn't stop Julie London, did it?"

"Herrick said you might make it with the proper handling."

"That's what I think." She turned from the hips, very serious now. "And I've got an idea. I've got a little money saved and I"—she faltered while something curious happened in the depths of her eyes before they cleared— "I think I can get a little more."

As though aware of this instant of hesitancy, she took a breath and continued with determination: "Somehow I'm going to get the right studio and the right engineer and the right audio set-up. I'm going to spend for a couple of arrangements and the proper backing—three or four pieces might be enough for my voice—and I'm going to have some tapes made. I know an agent who'll plug them for me if they're any good. If they're not—"

She stopped as though the thought was too discouraging to contemplate, and some of the enthusiasm died in her. She turned away, and just then the lobsters arrived and there was nothing more to be said.

The proper eating of a broiled lobster makes for no more than desultory conversation at best, and that was the way it happened this time. A word here, a word there, still on the subject of music; an agreement on some record, some performer, some melody. It was not until coffee had been served that Murdock thought of something else.

"What happens now?"

"To me? Florida."

"When?"

"Soon, I think. I'll send you a card when I have a place to live."

Murdock smiled indulgently before he realized she meant it. For she was already searching her bag and now she brought forth a tiny notebook with an attached pencil.

"Where do you live?"

He watched her write down the address, and it happened that he noticed his wrist watch. Having no idea the time had passed so quickly he suddenly thought of Charlie Lane and was dismayed to find that it was five minutes of nine. He put his napkin aside, caught the waiter's eye, and signaled for the check. It came almost at once and he put some bills down before he was conscious that the girl had been watching him. This time when she spoke her voice had a hint of softness in it that he had not noticed before.

"You know something," she said, still watching him. "You made one true statement over the phone this afternoon." She hesitated, her mouth curving. "You are a nice guy—and not just because you spent fourteen dollars buying my dinner. Men like you should have a club, an association of some kind. With merit badges so a girl could know in advance. I'm—sorry there can't be any 'on the town' because I know now I'd like it."

The simple compliment made Murdock feel good inside, but he was concerned with the time too, and he said: "This has been such good fun maybe we'd better quit while we're ahead."

"Yes," she said, with what sounded like a sigh. "I suppose so."

"I'm sorry you won't be around." Murdock moved the table back as she picked up her bag. "Of course I may be a bit old for you—"

She glanced up quickly and then saw his grin. "Poof!" she said. "You're not that old... Maybe you'll be in Florida some time this winter."

"I might at that."

"Will you look me up? Promise?"

Murdock said he would and they went out quickly then, saying nothing more until they were at the curb and a taxi swerved in and stopped. Murdock opened the door and when she was seated she leaned forward and offered her hand. He took it and she pulled slightly, and as he bent forward she gave him a quick kiss on the mouth before she released his hand.

CHAPTER 14

IT WAS six minutes after nine when Murdock hurried into the studio anteroom. There was no one in sight, so he continued on to his office and snapped on the light. The sheet of paper lay in the center of his blotting pad and he bent down to read the message, which was brief and somewhat cryptic:

Charlie Lane said to forget it. He changed his mind.

There was no time noted, no signature, and now Murdock flipped the switch on the two-way intercom that connected his office with the darkroom cubicles.

"Anybody in there?" he demanded.

"Me," said a voice filtered beyond recognition.

"Who's me?"

"Bailey."

"Did you write this note for me?"

"Yep."

"When?"

"About five minutes ago."

"Is that all there was to it?"

"That's all. I wrote down what the guy said and he hung up."

Murdock closed the circuit and sat down, his dark gaze unhappy and a feeling of frustration working on him. He examined the note again with some impatience and pushed it away. He was disgusted with himself, not because he thought his failure to be here was important but because he had let a pretty girl make him forget a promise.

"The hell with it," he said under his breath. Charlie Lane had actually made no promise at all. He had simply changed his mind. So what?

"Hello," he said, when he had the city desk. "Quiet tonight?"

"So far," the desk man replied. "I thought you'd gone home."

"I just stopped in for a minute. Bailey's here if you need anyone."

He hung up and got a cigarette going. It was time to go home but still he stayed. He puffed absently and this brought a bad taste to his mouth, and now the brooding inside him was getting worse. He swore again and wished there was a way to get Charlie on the telephone. He tried to dismiss the whole idea but the guilt remained, and suddenly he knew he had to have a better answer than that. He looked up the address Charlie had given him and visualized the location as being not too far from Scollay Square. A glance at the monitor told him that only one car was in use, so he asked for the city desk again and said he was going to take a car for a half hour and did it make any difference which one he took.

"They all need work on them so help yourself. Better check the radio with me before you start."

Murdock stood and snapped off the light. He unlocked the metal cabinet opposite his door, took out a camera and a small bag, relocked the cabinet, and headed for the elevator.

The address that Charlie Lane had given him was on the wrong side of the Hill, the street narrow and one-way as it led upward toward the State House. The ancient brick houses were built flush with the sidewalk, the doorways recessed for the most part, the flat roofs making a series of outsized steps against the night sky so that it was difficult to tell one from the other.

Murdock parked where he could and cramped the wheel so the tires snubbed against the curbing. When he had locked the doors he crossed to the nearest doorway and found that the next house was probably the one he sought. As he backed down the step and turned that way a man came out of the entrance.

He was hardly twenty-five feet away, but the darkness was so thick that he was no more than a vague figure without form or size. He seemed in that moment to glance toward Murdock and then wheel away as Murdock advanced. There was the sound of his steps on the sidewalk, which formed a faster counterpoint to Murdock's own, and then, unaccountably, he was gone.

Murdock did not know where, nor did he give the disappearance much thought. He did not think the other had reached the next doorway but he thought he saw an opening of some kind between the buildings. By then he had reached the entrance he sought and now he climbed the two steps and pushed open the door, which stood ajar. The hall beyond was narrow, with a staircase standing against one wall and mounting straight ahead in the semidarkness. There was a door just in front of the stairs, another opposite, and he could see the gleam of the wall telephone at the end of the narrow hall that bypassed the stairs.

The treads protested loudly as Murdock climbed, and he was conscious now of the acrid, musty smell that had permeated the building. Noises came from behind closed doors on the second floor landing: a woman's whine, an ugly oath, the loud distorted sound of music from a cheap radio. The stair treads still protested and the bannister creaked when he tested it.

The number Charlie Lane had given him was five, and this stood on the right of the next landing. Murdock knocked twice, listened, then tried the knob. The lock was the old-fashioned kind and the bolt had not been turned, so the panel swung easily, and now he had a quick picture of a squarish, depressing room with an iron bedstead, before his eyes focused on Charlie Lane, who sat with his head and shoulders slumped across a green-painted table.

Because the light was poor, Murdock took another step and said: "Charlie."

Then, even as he spoke, his gaze focused on the dark stain above one ear. He saw the red trickle on the side of the face, and now the horror struck at him, the shock holding him stiff, immobile, and incredulous.

It was a second at most that he stood there like that and by some odd chemistry of the mind he saw a different picture. He saw a sunburned, good-natured face and the easy grin that Charlie always had. He saw the bent figure trudging ahead on the golf course under the burden of two bags, and now remembered anecdotes and words of advice came back to him to make the shock and horror all the worse.

He said: "Charlie!" again and did not know he had spoken.

A sickness came to clog his throat and then, aware that the trickle was a moving thing that snaked its ugly way along the jaw, he remembered the man he had seen, the shadowy figure who had turned away from him and so mysteriously disappeared.

He moved quickly then, not with logic or great sense but understanding that this thing had happened very recently and seeking relief in action lest he dwell too long upon the fact that he had been too late.

Once outside the door he went down the ancient stairway three steps at a time, his hand sliding along the sticky bannister. He made it all in one breath and gulped deeply when he hit the sidewalk. Pivoting to the right he found the opening he thought was there, an alleyway of sorts, not wide enough for a vehicle but roughly paved.

Before he had taken three strides the blackness had blinded him. No longer had he any sense of direction and he had to put out one hand to find a brick wall and steady himself. The minute he stopped he realized that what he had done was foolish. He knew somehow that Charlie Lane had been shot. He had seen no gun. He could not tell where the alley went or how it ended, and as reason returned he held his breath again and that was when he heard the sound.

In that same instant his muscles froze and a sudden fear came to finger his thoughts and pluck at his nerve-ends. It was an insidious, paralyzing fear that grew when he recognized that sound—a labored breathing, not his own but close by and somewhere diagonally to his right.

It came distinctly now. It stayed constant and unmoving, and the harsh rhythm of it seemed to grow louder as his imagination took flight.

Someone was waiting, watching; someone whose eyes were far better adjusted to the darkness than his own. With a tremendous effort he broke the spell that held him immobile. He turned an inch at a time, the perspiration drying coldly on his spine. It took an added effort to pull his hand away from the wall. He tried to penetrate that barrier of darkness and could not. A glance over his shoulder revealed dimly the sidewalk opening and he wondered if he should try to back out. Then a strange anger came to counteract his fears and he swore silently and called himself a fool.

Exploring fingers found his cigarette lighter and he held it to one side at arm's length. If there was to be a shot it might be directed at the light and that should give him time enough because that sound of breathing was still close. He shifted his weight to the balls of his feet, crouching slightly before his thumb flicked the metal wheel.

The flash of flame located the source of the breathing, and there was no shot as Murdock stared and his eyes picked out the figure of a man who sat five feet diagonally ahead of him, the legs pulled up and the chin resting on the knees.

It took some seconds for Murdock to move, to get the tension out of his back and legs. He held the lighter slightly above his head and stepped forward to bend over a jackknifed figure that reeked of sweat and cheap wine. One hand clung loosely to an empty bottle, and when Murdock shook the limp shoulder the bottle rolled away.

Murdock said: "Hey," and shook again and the man said: "Wha—" without lifting his head. The mumble that followed was incoherent and animal-like in its inflection but the suggestion that he wanted to be left alone was apparent.

Aware now that there could be no point in asking the drunk if he had seen anyone come through the alley, Murdock put out the lighter and turned wearily back to the walk. At the doorway he hesitated, then continued on to his car, certain that with a wound of that sort Charlie Lane could not have lived long. The shock still lingered, but habit was strong and he unlocked the door of the company car automatically.

He started the motor to give added power to the radio, waited for the tubes to warm, and picked up the microphone. He thumbed the switch and said this was car eighty-two calling the *Courier*. When the answer came he related the brief facts and said he would call back.

"I'm going to stick with this," he said, "so send someone over for a filmholder. If I'm not in the car it will be on the front seat... And do this, will you? Keep after it until you get Lieutenant Bacon. Tell him this ties up with something he's already working on."

When he signed off he sat a moment listening to the faint chatter of the police calls on the other radio. He knew that presently there would be one which would send a car to this address, and now he reached for his camera, checked the filmholder, and put an extra bulb in his pocket. Once again the *Courier* morning editions would carry an exclusive picture of death, but this time Murdock had to force himself out of the car and into the house—because it was a job, because it was a thing he had to do while there was still time.

CHAPTER 15

KENT MURDOCK had just returned to his car with the exposed filmholder when a police cruiser sped by and braked quickly in front of him, the rear end sticking out into the street. The doors opened simultaneously and a uniformed officer stepped from each side. When Murdock moved out on the walk a flashlight beam hit him in the face and knifed past to sweep the company car.

"Newspaper car?" one man said.

"The *Courier*," Murdock said. "I'm Murdock."

"Oh, yeah. You found him, hunh? Where is he?"

"Room five, third floor."

"Let's go."

"I've seen him. I'd rather wait here for Homicide."

"You can wait with me. Come on... Get on the radio, Eddie," he said to his companion. "They'll probably have to block this street off at the bottom or we'll get all jammed up.

He motioned again to Murdock, and because he had no stomach for an argument, Murdock led the way until he reached the door which he had left ajar. He let the officer precede him and kept his eyes deliberately away from the still figure slumped over the table. There was a chair over against the wall beyond the bed and he headed for it, smelling the liquor now and locating the source as a pint bottle that had tipped over on the table.

A lieutenant and a detective from the precinct house were next to arrive, and after a brief huddle with the uniformed officer he withdrew. Murdock got a cigarette going, crossed his legs, and concentrated on the peeling wallpaper above the bed. He glanced briefly at the police photographer who arrived five minutes later with a camera and a huge equipment case. Occasionally a word came through to him and one that he heard repeated was:

Suicide.

He did not believe this but made no comment when an assistant medical examiner came in and got to work. Only two things seemed to matter and the thoughts kept repeating in his mind like a record with a stuck needle. Charlie Lane was dead and he might still be alive if he, Murdock, had been able to talk to him on the telephone at nine o'clock.

By now the room was a glare of light as the police specialist went about his job, and Murdock did not see Lieutenant Bacon come in; did not in fact know that he was there until, from out of the almost continuous welter of words, he heard the familiar voice. When he glanced round Bacon was talking to the examiner, who had already packed his bag and was putting on his coat. This time the words penetrated.

"Can't tell if it's a contact wound," the examiner was saying, "until we do the p.m. and shave that area. But the tattoo marks are there. The gun was awfully close."

Under his breath Murdock said: "They're all nuts," but he stayed where he was until the photographer's lights started to go out. He looked away once more when two ambulance attendants came by him with a basket stretcher and canvas and straps. He could hear them grunt as they worked, and then the room seemed stiller and there was only Bacon and the precinct men and himself.

Bacon picked up the only other chair in the room and brought it over toward Murdock. He sat down, his gray felt still centered on his head, his mouth grim and his eyes grave and intent.

"This is the guy from the motel," he said, making the words sound like a statement rather than a question. "The one that was with you when you found the woman?"

"Yes."

"How come you happened to be here at all?"

"He was supposed to call me at nine o'clock. I was a little late and he left word. I got worried and came over."

"Because you thought he was going to knock himself off?"

"I don't think he did."

"So we'll skip that part. What was he supposed to call you about?"

Murdock knew he had to be explicit now and he knew what Bacon's reaction would be. But because this no longer mattered, he spoke of his talk with Charlie Lane that noon and continued doggedly to the end.

Bacon did not interrupt but his voice was blunt and accusing when he spoke.

"You couldn't have come to me, could you? You had to try to play this one all by yourself. Something was eating the guy, and you knew it, and still you—"

"It wasn't my decision," Murdock yelled, as the crack in his self-control widened. "I went to T. A. Wyman. He said we ought to get Charlie to talk. If he had information you wanted we'd pass it along. I told him if he knew who killed Hazel Franklin he should go to you and he said he didn't know... But he must have known," he said. "He must have lied. Why else would anyone come here and kill him?"

He was looking right at Bacon as he spoke and he saw the look of surprise in the lieutenant's gray eyes. He thought Bacon was about to reply because he opened his mouth; instead he closed it, hesitated, and tried again.

"What was the message he left tonight?" He listened as Murdock repeated it. "How much money did he want this noon?"

"He said he'd like to get two fifty. He wanted money to get to Florida."

"Well—his bags were packed."

Bacon gestured toward two suitcases near one wall.

They stood open now, but Murdock did not know if they had been found that way or whether the detectives had opened them.

"You didn't touch him?" the lieutenant continued. "Or anything in the room?"

Murdock shook his head. He said he knew it must have just happened because he had seen the blood trickling down the face. And then he remembered the man on the sidewalk and he straightened in his chair and spoke quickly as his mind recaptured the incident. He told of his chase and the drunk in the alley.

"That could have been the guy," he said. "Five minutes earlier and I could have nailed him—or maybe even stopped it... Five minutes," he said miserably, his bitterness turned inward, "and I had to be late."

"Maybe five minutes would have made a difference," Bacon said quietly. "But there wasn't any other guy. Lane shot himself."

Murdock heard each word distinctly, but something inside him rebelled and he shook his head, his dark gaze outraged and incredulous.

"You're crazy. Why the hell should he do that?"

Bacon pointed at the table and Murdock saw the gun there.

"A German automatic," Bacon said. "A Mauser, probably a war souvenir. It was at his feet. The wound was either contact or very close to it."

"So what? Things like this have been framed before."

Bacon made no reply but reached into his pocket. Very carefully then he took out a platinum-and-diamond wrist watch and spread it across a bony knee. He added a diamond solitaire. Finally he produced a pawn ticket.

"This"—he tapped the ticket—"was in his pocket. The other stuff was in one of the bags."

Murdock looked at the exhibits, his eyes wide open and the amazement growing in them. Until that moment he had been too emotionally upset and too conscious of his own possible guilt to think constructively or even to reason with any great convincingness. Now, because he refused to accept the conclusion that Bacon presented, he found alternatives and began to argue them with some heat.

"That jewelry had already been taken when Charlie and I found her," he said.

"Sure," Bacon said. "Because he only pretended to find her when you crabbed about that radio playing. He took this stuff a long time before that—when he strangled her."

"No."

"Don't ask exactly how it happened because I can't tell you." Bacon replaced the jewelry and the ticket. "I don't say he killed to get those pieces. He might have been lifting something else and she caught him and started to yell and he used the stocking to silence her. Once he realized she was dead he decided to take the stuff and—"

Murdock cut him off. "Wait a minute. Wait just a minute... If he had that jewelry all the time, why try to get two hundred and fifty bucks out of the Courier? Why bother with me?"

"Because," Bacon said with remarkable patience for him, "the jewelry was hot. If he could get transportation out of you he'd be a lot safer disposing of it in Florida, wouldn't he?"

"But he didn't get the money," Murdock argued. "He pawned a ring."

"Because you scared him off. You told him he ought to come to us. You didn't buy the deal. You stalled him."

"How much money did he have on him?"

"Two hundred and ten dollars."

Murdock recalled again the twenty-dollar bills Charlie Lane had when he got the ten-dollar tip on the golf course. He had thought at the time that Lane had about seventy dollars, even though Chief Nickerson said he had recently been cleaned at a race track.

"How much is the pawn ticket for?"

"One sixty."

Murdock took a breath and blew it out. His bony face was set and shiny and the stubborn glints were still in his eyes.

"All right. Then why should he kill himself?"

"Because it got too big for him. He lost his courage."

Bacon leaned forward to accent his words. "He pawned the ring—maybe he was a little drunk at the time—and tonight he sat here drinking alone and worrying about you and knowing that once we located that ring—and we'd have had the report in the morning— he was cooked. He was through and he knew it and he took the easy way out. If you weren't so goddamned guilt-ridden," he added impatiently, "you'd admit it... How often did you see him?"

"Three or four times a summer."

"For how long?"

"I don't know. Four or five years."

"You liked him. Because he was a good caddy and you got some laughs. He was a character. He was a bum."

"Oh, no," Murdock said resentfully.

"He was nearly as old as I am but he was still a caddy," said Bacon, who was no golfer. "Summers in the north, winters in Florida. He blew his money on liquor and horses and lived in cribs like this." He waved an arm to indicate the room, the house, and its environs.

"What's wrong with being a caddy?"

"Nothing," said Bacon, taken back by Murdock's vehemence.

"Or playing the horses? He paid his way. He earned his money. Not like some I know of who work here six or seven months and then take off for Florida and collect unemployment insurance while they sit around in the sun at our expense."

Bacon uttered a small sigh and felt his hat to make sure it was on straight. He glanced round at the others in the room, who had been poking into this and that and listening with one ear. He put his hands on his knees, as though getting ready to rise, and gave a small shake to his head. Bacon had been a policeman for a great many years and he played by the book. He was shrewd, competent, experienced, and he was jealous of his authority and his prerogatives. There had been times when he had been outraged by things Murdock had done and he was by nature suspicious. But he also understood the photographer and knew that their association had flourished because of a mutual respect.

He had no desire to continue the argument or point out the errors of judgment Murdock had made because he knew Murdock was already too aware of them. Murdock had been hard hit by the tragedy and, because he understood so well, Bacon stepped out of character for a brief moment and his voice was sympathetic.

"Okay," he said and stood up. "You want to argue we can do it tomorrow. Right now you'd better come along and give us a brief statement. Come on."

He waited until Murdock rose, then touched his arm to steer him toward the door. "It won't take long," he said. "Then you can go home and get drunk if you want to."

CHAPTER 16

KENT MURDOCK was not very observant when he entered his apartment at eleven o'clock that evening. He was in no mood to be observant about anything, and as he closed the door his glance moved to his record player and he thought of something that in the past had always acted as an antidote to his occasional depressions.

He brought forth an old album that had the unlikely title of Chamber Music Society of Lower Basin Street. The selections were old standards, the renditions equally divided between Dr. Henry (Hot-lips) Levine and his Barefooted Dixieland Philharmonic, and Maestro Paul Laval and his Wood-wind Ten. The program comments were made in a Metropolitan Opera House manner by Dr. Gino Hamilton, and when the music came Murdock remembered how faithfully he used to follow that program on the radio. Why the hell was it, he asked himself morosely, that a guy couldn't get music like that on the air anymore? No sponsors smart enough to back a program like this—or too smart because they thought the appeal was so limited?

The only thing good he had seen on television was that hour program CBS had put on one Sunday afternoon. It was called the "Sound of Jazz," or something like that. Count Basie and Billie Holliday and three or four smaller groups. No scenery, no dancing girls, no special effects. Just about twenty "mikes," a good audio man to co-ordinate them, and a bunch of guys blowing their brains out with not a sheet of music in the studio.

He turned away, still grumbling silently, to get the drink he wanted. That was when he noticed something different about the kneehole desk by the wall. He was not sure why it seemed different but when he stepped over to it and opened the center drawer he knew instinct had been right. The papers here were a tangled mess and other drawers bore out the conclusion that the desk had been thoroughly searched.

Leaning stiff-armed on the top, he stared sightlessly at the wall beyond, his mind confused and suspicious, until he became aware of a sense of warmth that had nothing to do with his thoughts. He brought his glance to focus and it moved just beyond one arm to the desk lamp. On impulse he touched the metal reflector, then the bulb. The bulb was cold, or nearly so—he was not sure—but there was a definite warmth to the reflector, slight but unmistakable. He straightened slowly, dark eyes on the move and his senses suddenly alert and sharply tuned. He had no idea how long such a reflector would hold the heat, but he understood there was a chance the one who had searched the desk was still here.

There was a coat closet just inside the door and he went there first. When he found it empty he thought about his darkroom and headed for the kitchen. At the door he stopped to listen. When he could hear nothing but the faint thudding of his pulse, he reached inside and snapped on the light.

The kitchen was empty. So was the darkroom.

He put out the light and wheeled toward the bedroom.

At the door he stopped again to listen and then flicked the switch. The first glance told him nothing at all. From where he stood everything seemed in order and he was about to retreat when he saw the bathroom door. It was closed. But not by him.

Living alone as he did, he never closed it. Warned by such knowledge, the pressure that had been building inside him came swiftly to a head. His gaze still fixed on that closed door, he stepped to the bedside table and took out a .32 automatic that he had kept for many years.

He never left a bullet in the chamber but he jacked one into place now and kept on moving. It was his plan to throw open the door suddenly and step back to see what happened next. The gun was level in his right hand as he reached for the knob. As he touched it, he twisted and pushed hard; then bumped into a panel that would not move.

He tried again to be sure it was locked. He stepped back.

"Come on out!" he yelled angrily. "With your hands up."

In the other room the record was spinning out a smooth and expert rendition of "Runnin Wild," but the only answer Murdock got was the sound of a toilet flushing. For some reason this served only to infuriate him and he banged the door again, getting no answer but hearing the faint sound of the bowl filling up.

When this stopped the toilet flushed again and, like that, an answer came to Murdock and he backed up to the chest. One eye on the door, he reached down and pulled out the bottom drawer. Then he knew the letters he had hidden there were gone.

A glance at the bed told him it had not been touched and he knew the two films he had taken of the letters must still be there. It gave him a sort of vindictive satisfaction to know this and his gaze was darkly brooding as he watched the bathroom door open and saw Paul Herrick step out.

The tall broad-shouldered figure was immaculate in a light-brown suit. The handsome face with the close-set ears and the cleft in the chin was at ease and the brown eyes seemed unworried as they fastened on the gun.

"You won't need that now. If you want to call the police go ahead."

"If I'd plugged you through that door," Murdock said, "you wouldn't be so cocky."

"It was a chance I had to take."

Murdock backed to the door and into the other room.

When he motioned with the gun, Herrick followed. He sat down in the club chair, made a small production of selecting a cigarette from a silver case and getting a light. He leaned back and crossed his legs.

"I didn't have much choice," he said finally. "I spent three hours this afternoon at police headquarters. They kept banging away at me because they knew that Hazel was my girl for a while. With those letters they'd have a motive."

"I could have turned them in yesterday," Murdock said. "Not without giving an explanation that might have been awkward for you. I don't think you held out because we're buddies."

There was some truth in what Herrick said and Murdock admitted it. That there had been other reasons was unirnportant now.

"How did you know I had them?"

Herrick chuckled softly and waved the cigarette. "A smart fellow like you should be able to figure that out."

"You're the one who jumped me in her bedroom."

"You walked in on me before I'd finished. I had to get out."

"How'd you get in?"

"The same way you did, I guess. The same way I got in here tonight."

"You waited outside after you left," Murdock said, as the answers began to fall into place.

"I was parked down the street. Pretty soon I saw the police car pull in front of the place, so I kept on waiting."

He inhaled and said: "Not long after that you came round the corner and got into your car. I had to figure the police would search that apartment either yesterday or today. If they had found the letters they'd have hit me over the head with them. So"—he shrugged with his hands—"they didn't find them. That left you... Incidentally that's a terrific record you've got on. You don't hear Basin Street played like that very often."

Murdock agreed silently and he also was nettled by Herrick's attitude. Real or simulated, his indifference seemed supreme, and when Murdock had switched off the record he sat down and said:

"I also forgot to tell the police I saw you driving out of the Pine Grove Motel around nine thirty Saturday night."

The effect of the statement was satisfactory. Herrick's smile vanished and his eyes were suddenly clouded with doubt. He narrowed them slightly and his hps flattened. "Who says so besides you?"

"Nobody. Unless the police find someone else who saw you it's your word against mine, but don't get the idea you're in the clear."

He paused, thinking again of Charlie Lane but having no stomach to discuss his death with Herrick.

"It's a pity you had to get rid of those letters in such a hurry," he said.

"What do you mean, it's a pity?"

"If I had been a little later, if you'd taken them home and had a chance to study them, you might have noticed something different about two of them."

Herrick forgot about his cigarette. The doubt in his eyes gave way to concern and the tanned forehead was suddenly grooved.

"Different?"

"Different," Murdock said. "You just might have noticed a tiny hole in each corner of those two letters, two more holes in the envelopes."

He leaned forward slightly, still holding the gun.

"Those letters worried me," he said. "I couldn't decide whether to turn them over to the police or not. I thought I might even return them if they found another boy to fit that murder. But in my business you get the habit of recording things on film, all sorts of things."

Herrick got the message. He was having trouble accepting it but he put his feet flat on the floor and there were dangerous glints in his eyes.

"You made copies of them?" he asked softly.

"I photographed two of them. Blown up and reproduced, they'll be as good for evidence as the originals."

Herrick rose slowly, spotted an ash tray and dropped the cigarette. He moved his lips silently and his gaze flicked round the room and came back to Murdock. He seemed in that moment to be measuring the distance that separated him from the gun, to be weighing the odds.

"Where are they?"

He waited. When he got nothing but a silent stare from Murdock he said: "If you didn't have that gun I'd take you and then I'd take this place apart." Hesitating, his fingers working at his sides, he added: "I've got something wonderful working for me and I'll do what I have to do to keep it that way."

"Even a stretch for assault?"

"I'd rather take a chance on that than have my girl know about those letters I wrote to Hazel. I must have been out of my mind. Maybe I still am."

He stopped and Murdock moved over to open the door.

He was very uncomfortable holding that gun. He had no intention of using it to shoot with but he knew it might happen if Herrick jumped him. He gestured with it.

"I don't like this either," he said. "But you're a few years younger, four inches taller, and fifty pounds heavier, so I ought to have a little something extra."

He took the automatic with his left hand, fitted it into the palm of his right so that it lay flat and snug. He was ready to swing then and he stood there poised and waiting and half hoping that Herrick would accept the challenge.

"You broke in here," he said flatly. "That much I'll let you get away with. If you think you can take me, try it. If not, get out."

Herrick took a breath and his shoulders seemed to bulge a little. He pressed his right fist into the palm of his other hand and his light-brown eyes were suddenly crafty.

"Okay," he said and started past Murdock. One step from the door he wheeled and swung the right in a quick vicious punch that would have floored Murdock if he had not been warned by the look he had seen.

It was not a clever move because it was a roundhouse punch that started too far back and took too much time. Murdock pulled his chin back. The fist missed by two inches, the force of the blow pulling the big man off balance, and leaving his shoulders and head partly turned. Before he could recover, Murdock stepped in and slammed the side of the gun against the side of Herrick's head, not savagely but with authority.

Herrick staggered and took another step. This brought him almost to the doorway. He put his hand up to his ear. His handsome face was twisted and pale at the jaw and when he hesitated he seemed to understand it was too late. He had had his chance and it missed. Murdock was still there, still waiting. Any further attempt would have to be made head-on and Herrick apparently decided against it. He spun about and walked through the opening.

CHAPTER 17

WHEN MURDOCK was sure the door was locked he went back to the record player to play the other sides. For a minute he simply stood and listened, liking what he heard and feeling his muscles relax. He tried very hard not to think about Herrick or Charlie Lane and when he remembered the gun he removed the clip, ejected the shell, retrieved it from the carpet, wiped it off, and inserted it in the clip.

Back in the bedroom he replaced the gun and took off his jacket. He substituted slippers for shoes, removed his tie and unbuttoned his collar. He got a cigarette going and went directly to the kitchen for the drink that had been too long delayed. He poured generously from the whisky bottle, found some loose ice cubes in a tray that was partly empty. When he had added water from the faucet, he took a big swallow and said: "Ahh—"

Henry (Hot-lips) Levine was riding a neat chorus when he came into the living room and he turned the volume down slightly before he went to the telephone and dialed the *Courier* number. He thought this might be a good time to catch the entertainment editor, who made his own hours, and when the operator told him Neil Randall was in the building he asked to be connected.

"Neil?" he said. "Kent Murdock. Do you know a musician named Paul Herrick?"

"Sure. Plays piano good."

"I think he's opening in a week at the Melody Grill and I wonder if you could snoop around a bit and find out how he's fixed for dough."

"You want to borrow some?"

"I want to know if Herrick has any. You might hear some gossip that would give you a clue. You may draw a blank, but I'd appreciate it if you'd give it a try."

"Sure. I'll ask around. You in a hurry?"

"If you haven't got anything by tomorrow afternoon forget it. I'll call you then."

He looked up another number, dialed. "Sherlock?" he said when a voice answered.

"Mr. Holmes to you, sir. Who's this?"

"Murdock."

"Well, well. The camera kid himself. Where've you been keeping yourself?"

Jack Fenner was a long-time friend of Murdock's. More important now was the fact that he was probably the best private detective in town. He was the man who had given Murdock the thin steel blade that was useful for opening certain types of doors and there had been times in the past when Fenner had done some work for the *Courier*.

"I've been around," Murdock said. "And I've got a little job for you."

"I know just the kind of job," Fenner said. "You want me to crack a bank or slug somebody, but I'll have to do it cheap because I'll be doing it for you and you're not holding much cash."

Murdock laughed and said Fenner was partly right.

"Especially about the cash part." He went on to speak of Paul Herrick and explain what he wanted to know. "I don't know where he lives but he's opening a week from Monday, so he's got to live some place. You could check with the union. They ought to know. I'd like to find out if he has any money in the bank."

"What bank?"

"I don't know."

"Hah. What am I, a magician?"

"You can try. You know everybody, don't you?"

"Not bankers."

"Well, will you try? Will you do the best you can?"

Sure.

"How much will it cost me?"

"Fifty bucks a day."

"I want the discount rate."

"Forty."

"Eight hours?"

"Right."

"Okay, but split the eight up where it will do the most good, will you? If I don't call you tomorrow afternoon, call the office."

He hung up and went back to his chair before he realized that The Chamber Music Society of Lower Basin Street had finished its engagement. The record was spinning silently and he turned off the machine and took a gulp of his drink. As he put the glass down the buzzer startled him.

The unexpected sound offended him and he glared at the door, as though by wishing he could make the visitor go away. When the buzzer sounded again he glanced at his watch and saw that it was ten minutes of twelve. Then he thought about Paul Herrick, and the gun in the bedside table. He wanted no more of Herrick tonight. By now Herrick's mood would be both unpredictable and dangerous but—

Herrick wouldn't come back. Why should he when he knew Murdock still had a gun? This is what he told himself as he started for the door, but as a precautionary measure he picked up the heavy bronze ash tray that stood on the small table at one side. Holding it solidly in his right hand and keeping the hand behind one hip, he planted his foot six inches in front of the door to stop it in case someone tried to force it. He turned the knob to give it a short smart jerk and then he was staring foolishly through the opening at Lucille Dunn.

She looked just as pretty as ever and she had the same black dress and cloth coat that she had worn at dinner. The only thing different was the black-leather overnight case she held in one hand.

Murdock recovered slowly and he had no words. He opened the door, still feeling foolish about his precautions and finding the ash tray very heavy in his hand.

"Well," Lucille said. "Aren't you going to ask me in?"

"Sure." Murdock backed up obliquely and got rid of the ash tray. "Sure," he said. "It's just that I don't get many surprises like this."

She put the bag down inside the door and walked past, letting him close it. She gave the room a brief but thorough inspection, her glance touching the chairs, the divan, the sporting prints on the walls, the books.

"It's real nice," she said judiciously. "Of course a woman could brighten it up here and there but I guess you're comfortable."

Murdock was still confused. He continued to gawk at her as she slipped off her coat and tossed it onto a chair. She felt her hair and then turned, her smile bright and a certain coquettishness in her manner he had not seen before.

"I thought I might stay here tonight," she said, "if you have room for me?" She tipped her head, the blue eyes very active and the lashes busy. "What's the matter? I thought you liked me."

"I do."

"But you seem so suspicious."

"I am suspicious."

"But—"

"The last time you gave me the glad eye and the innocent approach I lost two films. I almost lost my car."

"Oh—that." She dismissed the thought. "I didn't know you then." She gestured idly. "You do have room, don't you?"

Murdock understood no part of the routine. He only knew the act was unconvincing. To see if he could find out the reason for it he decided to shake her up a bit.

"Sure I've got room, baby." He stepped up to her and put his hands on her arms and pulled her close. "I have a very comfortable double bed. Do you want to get undressed and put on a robe now or have a couple of drinks first?"

He could feel her stiffen and pull back. The blue eyes opened wide and were suddenly uncertain and a little afraid. But she did very well under the circumstances. She kept her voice controlled. She brought forth some laughter as she twisted free and stepped to the divan.

"I didn't mean that, exactly. I wouldn't think of taking your bed." She felt the cushions and sat down. She bounced experimentally. "This is just my size. This will be wonderful."

Murdock followed her. He sat down next to her, his dark gaze amused but still puzzled. He slipped his arm around her but did not tighten it.

"I guess your deal went through."

"What deal?"

"You couldn't go out on the town with me. You had a date. You walk in here with your bag packed. Does that mean you're off for Florida?"

She nodded, her eyes fixed straight ahead.

"When?"

"In the morning. My bags are already at the airport."

"And you want a sack for tonight? What happened at the Lynn? Get tired of that room?"

"Sort of."

"There are other hotels. You're not broke, are you?"

"Oh, heavens, no."

"You just came here because you like me."

"That and—well, I decided tonight I could trust you and—"

She broke off, her voice faltering. For the first time she seemed to be forgetting her lines and Murdock, believing no part of what he had heard, decided to crowd her.

He tightened his arm slightly, turning her torso a little as he pressed closer. She was still staring straight ahead and her red mouth was set. She did not resist but he felt the tension in her. He also knew she had very firm breasts or that the brassiere was very tight, compacting the fullness so that it felt hard against his chest. He kissed her cheek and brushed his lips against her ear. He kept them there as he spoke.

"I've got a proposition," he said. "It's better than most because you've got a choice. We can use my very comfortable bed and there'll be no more questions. There doesn't even have to be any talk."

He felt the tension grow in the young body as he hesitated and now he said:

"Or, if you want to start being honest with me and tell me why you came here and put on the act, you can have the bed yourself and a key to the door if you think you need it."

He took his lips away from her ear. The fragrance of her hair and skin was in the back of his throat now and he found himself wishing that she was a little older and the circumstances were different. He could feel her body start to relax and was conscious of the swelling of her bosom as she took a breath. Very gently then she disengaged herself and now the blue eyes were inspecting his face.

"All right," she said and sighed softly. "I guess that's fair enough. But could I have one of those first?"

She pointed at his half-filled glass and Murdock pushed up from the divan. He said Scotch, and she said, yes, please, and he went out to the kitchen to get the drink. When he came back she had a cigarette lighted and her pretty knees were crossed. She drank gratefully from her glass.

"I was scared," she said. "That's why I came. I meant it when I said I knew I could trust you. You were kidding, weren't you, when you said I could take off my clothes?"

"It was just a thought," Murdock said. "You're not a very good actress yet."

"I know," she said, and sighed again.

He swallowed some of his drink and leaned back. After a few seconds she continued.

"Someone tried to get into my room tonight."

Murdock eyed her narrowly, one brow lifting, and then he knew that this was no longer any act. The concern in her voice was convincing and he paid attention.

"It was about a quarter after eleven. I'd just had a bath and the light was out in the room because I intended to go right to bed. I walked out of the bathroom with nothing but a towel and I heard this funny noise. I didn't know what it was but it seemed to come from the door, so I moved a little closer. Somehow the light from the bathroom fell on the door just right and that's how I saw the key."

She took another sip and said: "It's an old hotel and the locks are old and the keys are big and you have to lock yourself in. What I heard was the key. It was moving. I saw it turning. I was too petrified to do anything but watch—until it fell out on the floor. When I heard someone start to use another key from the outside, I pounded on the door and snapped on the light. I said if he didn't go away I'd scream. I guess I was pretty nearly screaming then because the key went away."

"If who didn't go away?"

"What?" she said, not understanding.

"You said: 'He.'"

"Well—a woman wouldn't be doing it, would she?"

Murdock thought it over, no longer doubting her and searching for some answer.

"It could have been some drunk."

"No. A drunk would have made some noise. There wasn't any. Just the sound of that key." She shivered unconsciously. "I can still hear it. I knew whoever had done it had gone, but how could I tell he might not come back after I'd gone to sleep... And then I knew I didn't dare go to sleep."

She looked at him, her tanned face puckered a little in her effort to convince him.

"Maybe you think I scare easy. Maybe you think I'm a nitwit, and maybe I am. But the way I felt then I knew I had to get out of that room. I dressed and packed my bag. I phoned down for a bellboy and stayed right with him until he got me a cab. And then I thought: Suppose the man is still waiting? Suppose he's watching me now? He could follow me to another hotel, couldn't he? And I wouldn't be any better off there... That's when I thought of you."

Murdock smiled at her. He knew her fears were genuine —at least to her. "I must have made quite a good impression at dinner."

"Better than you know."

He drained his glass and stood up to get a refill. In the kitchen, away from the girl's distracting influence, he put his mind to work. Presently he came up with a possible explanation, but before he could voice it she changed the subject.

She was fishing through her handbag as he approached the divan and now she brought forth a small bright object and presented it to him.

"I think this is yours."

It was a gold tie-clip and the minute he saw it he recognized it.

"Where'd you get it?"

"Just outside my cottage. On the grass." She hesitated, her small smile embarrassed. "You know— where Felix and Nate put you out."

"Threw me out," Murdock corrected.

"I guess they did, didn't they? Well, Felix saw it the next morning before I left. He said it was probably yours. He said he didn't expect to see you again but I might."

Murdock turned it over in his fingers and put it on the end table. There was something here that bothered him. He did not know whether it was the thought of the clip itself, or the story she told. He only knew that certain vague details were in conflict, but because this new thought of his seemed more important he speculated no more about the clip.

"Tell me," he said. "Were you at the Pine Grove Motel at any time Saturday night?"

"Why—yes."

"For what reason?"

"I knew a man who was staying there. From Maine. He was on his way to New York and he stopped there because he thought he could date me. I told him I had to work and Saturday night would be busy and after that I had to pack. I did go there to have a couple of drinks with him. I borrowed Felix's car."

"What time did you get there?"

"About seven."

"When did you leave?"

"Oh—maybe a quarter after eight or so."

"Who did you see?"

The tanned brow was still furrowed and the blue eyes seemed puzzled beneath the mascaraed lashes.

"Lots of people. You always do around motels—going for ice and soda to the main building or to the lunchroom or unpacking cars."

"Men?"

"I saw three or four."

"I'm talking about the last cottage on the right. It was nearly dark, wasn't it? And you had your headlights on when you left?"

"Yes."

"And you saw someone going into or out of that last cottage."

"I don't remember."

"Some man hanging around there then."

"I could have. Maybe I did."

Murdock studied her face and it told him nothing. She sounded as if she were telling the truth, or trying to. She seemed genuinely sincere but he hated to give up.

"But if you did see—"

"Oh, now, really," she cut in. "You just don't pay any attention to people when you're in a car—unless there's something very unusual about them."

"Then you didn't see anyone you recognized?"

She leaned forward and took her glass from the coffee table. She took two small swallows and put the glass back. When she was ready she said:

"No. I didn't."

Murdock sighed heavily. He was through with this phase and he knew it. He also knew he was getting very, very sleepy. He had to make a conscious effort to keep his eyes open. He could still think, though this too had become an effort, and he considered again this girl and the things that made her tick.

She was going to Florida, apparently having reached some decision since dinner. She had no job. In his opinion she was neither tough nor common and he did not think she would withhold evidence or perjure herself for money alone. But there might be other considerations more important to her.

The dominant force that was shaping her philosophy was her career. She wanted to sing and intended to keep trying so long as there was a chance for success. Carl Darrow had money in a night club in Miami Beach. He could offer her a job; if necessary he could promise her a chance to sing. Such things were important to her. She would listen to Darrow, try to please him.

There was also one other requisite for her future as a singer. She had to have the proper arrangements. They had to be right for her voice and her delivery. Such arrangements were expensive. Paul Herrick could make them. A promise like that would carry great weight. He, too, had worked in Florida. He might even have been able to promise her some sort of opening—

Murdock leaned forward and took two fast gulps from his glass in an effort to revive himself. He had a few more things to say before he turned his bedroom over to her, but as he leaned back he could not remember what they were. He could still smell her perfume and he knew she was close beside him but he could not seem to get the words out. He knew his eyelids had shut and he let them stay that way while he made one more effort to express himself. He groped for her and his hand found hers. He felt the warmth of her before his fingers slipped limply to the cushion. . . .

CHAPTER 18

IN HIS DREAM, Murdock heard the telephone ringing. It was a great distance away and there were long corridors intervening and he knew he had to hurry before the ringing stopped. The telephone was in sight now, but when he tried to reach it his arms were not long enough. He had to summon all his strength, to make one last desperate lunge. As he did so he fell heavily and the floor was beneath him and he opened his eyes.

The fall jarred him and in that first instant he thought he had fallen out of bed. Not until he glanced round and tried to lift his head did he realize that he was in the living room and that he had fallen not from his bed but from the divan.

The telephone was still ringing as he pushed himself to a sitting position and got one knee under him. He staggered erect, bewildered and groggy and uncertain of his balance. Somehow he made it to the little stand and groped for the instrument. He had to look to see which end was which and finally he made up his mind.

"Yeah," he said thickly. "Yeah."

"Kent? . . . Delaney. I just called to see if anything was wrong."

"No," Murdock said. "Nothing's wrong." He tried to swallow the horrible taste from his mouth and it stuck in his throat. "Why? What time is it?"

"Ten o'clock."

Murdock groaned aloud and wet his lips. "I took a pill last night," he said. "I just woke up. You got things under control?"

"Oh, sure. I just thought—"

"Hang on. I'll be along in a half hour or so."

He dropped the telephone into its cradle and ran his fingers through his tousled dark hair. He was still unsteady on his feet as he headed for the kitchen to put some water on for coffee. When he came back he looked down on the divan which had been his bed. His slippers lay beside it.

A thin blanket had covered him and the pillow apparently had come from the bedroom. He began disrobing as he started that way and he could see the note from the doorway. It had been left in the center of the counterpane, and as he reached for it he saw that the bed had been neatly made except for the missing pillow. The subtle fragrance of the bed's most recent tenant still lingered in the air as he began to read her handwriting.

Dear Kent:

I'm sorry I had to trick you but I really did have a flight reservation this morning and I had to be sure I made it. You were a bit argumentative, you know, and you were asking a lot of questions I wasn't sure I could answer. I wasn't sure I could handle you either. I really was scared last night, and that's why I came, and I'm glad I did. It wasn't a Micky I gave you but a mixture another girl told me about. In my business you have to go out with men sometimes. They're not always as nice as you and when they get difficult it's easiest if they sort of go to sleep quietly, if you know what I mean. But I will write you when I have an address and maybe you can come to Florida this winter.

Lucille.

Murdock put the note on the chest and finished his undressing. He was beginning to feel better and there was no resentment in his mind as it recaptured the details of the previous night. Nothing that happened had changed his original opinion that this was a smart and essentially nice girl who could think for herself when she had to. He let his thoughts expand as he shaved and stepped under the shower. As he toweled warmth into his skin he was ready to believe that there had been a man who had tried to get into her hotel room, but he also felt that she had had help in getting to Florida. He was still convinced that she had collaborated with Carl Darrow in an attempt to give him an alibi, and it was still very possible that she had also seen him at the Pine Grove Motel. Having helped him once it was understandable that she might he for him again.

In the kitchen he opened a can of tomato juice and laced a glass with salt and Worcestershire. The bread was almost gone but he salvaged a slice to drop in the toaster before he wrapped the heel and put it into the wastebasket. Disguised with butter and marmalade it tasted quite good and by the time he was sipping his second cup of coffee his head felt more normal and he was able to appreciate even more the girl's resourcefulness. That she was extremely easy on the eyes, both as to face and figure, added decidedly to his appreciation of her as a person and he grinned absently as he admitted that fact.

When he had rinsed his dishes he went back to the living room to straighten the divan and put the pillow and blanket away. It was then that he noticed the tie-clip on the end table.

He picked it up, certain now that it was his but wondering how it happened to be there. Gradually then the scene came back to him and he remembered the story she had told. He had lost it when he was thrown out of her cottage, and Felix had found it, but—

He checked the thought as a new one replaced it, and suddenly his gaze narrowed and became darkly speculative. For he already had a tie-clip. He had dropped it on the floor of the motel cottage and Charlie Lane had tossed it to him. Because he had seen that his clip was missing he had put it on and thought no more about it. So where the hell was it? What happened to it?

Back in the bedroom he inspected the leather stud box. No tie-clip. When had he used it last? He had worn a polo shirt for golf. He had changed into a clean one afterward when he had showered. He had not worn a tie until yesterday morning but neither had he emptied the leather duffel bag he had taken with him Saturday.

He brought it from the closet and hunkered down to pull the zipper. Then he took out a soiled shirt, a crumpled polo shirt, two dirty handkerchiefs, a pair of socks, a folder of matches advertising a bar, an automatic pencil, and a regimental-striped necktie.

The clip was at the very bottom and he remembered having tossed it there when he undressed early Sunday morning. Viewed closely he saw that the essential similarity between this clip and his own was the size and shape. If he had not been too occupied with murder and photographs on Saturday night he would have noticed the difference in design; if he had not been so exhausted, if it had not been after four in the morning when he took off his tie, he might have realized the truth then.

For this was a heavier clip than his. When he looked more closely and saw that it was marked 18k, his mistake was even more evident. But it was the design on the face that held his interest. The embossed lines that formed a squarish, overlapping pattern seemed vaguely familiar. He knew he had seen a similar design somewhere, and not too long ago. He turned the clip over and over in his fingers, but when the answer continued to escape him he pocketed it and finished dressing.

Delaney was sitting at Murdock's desk when he walked into the studio at a quarter of eleven. He said that everything was under control but that the Sunday editor wanted to talk to Murdock about a layout and that T. A. Wyman had asked for him.

Murdock thanked him, sat down, spun the dial to get an outside line and then worked on the number for police headquarters. He asked for Homicide but when he was connected the detective who answered said Lieutenant Bacon was out. Offering no information as to where Bacon might be, he did add that the lieutenant was expected back in about an hour.

Murdock kept busy during the next hour. He worked things out with the Sunday editor and got an okay on a layout. He talked for ten minutes with Wyman but when the managing editor heard Murdock's story he had a few suggestions to offer.

"We didn't print the piece as a suicide because we couldn't get a confirmation. The M.E.'s office said it looked like suicide but couldn't say pending an autopsy. The police wouldn't say anything. As of now your friend Charlie Lane was found dead under mysterious circumstances."

He rolled the cigar to the opposite corner of his mouth and said: "Why don't you go see your pal Bacon? Maybe you can talk him out of something we can print. If it's suicide let's give it a paragraph and forget it. If not"— he shrugged expressively—"maybe we've got a story."

Murdock said he would see what he could find out and he was waiting outside Bacon's office listening to two detectives question a woman who had been brought in as a material witness when the lieutenant came in at ten minutes of twelve. His grunt of recognition was something less than cordial but he offered no objection when Murdock rose and followed him into his office.

Bacon hung up his hat, opened the lone window an inch and a half, and sat down. He examined a report on his desk for a silent minute or two. He picked up the telephone and spoke in cryptic phrases about a case that held no interest for Murdock. When he was ready he leaned back, sighed, fixed his gray expressionless gaze on Murdock, and uttered another small uncommunicative grunt.

"What do you want?"

"I want to know what you found out about Charlie Lane's death."

"A lot of things."

Murdock sat down. This, he could tell from Bacon's present mood, was going to be a tedious session, but he was not discouraged. He had time and he knew if he could think of something that interested the lieutenant the mood could easily change.

"Like what?"

"He pawned the ring."

"The ticket was on him."

"It could have been planted, couldn't it? . . . Lane pawned it at four twenty yesterday afternoon, too late for a report unless the pawnbroker was especially suspicious. He wasn't."

"You still say it was suicide?"

"I'm not saying anything. I'm waiting for the final report from the medical examiner's office."

Bacon began to rock very gently in his chair, back and forth, back and forth, the sound that came from the spring control varying one note with each change of direction.

When Murdock got tired of waiting, he slumped in his chair and pushed his legs straight out, the ankles crossed.

"If you want to know what I think, I'll tell you."

"I don't want to know," Bacon retorted, not actually meaning it.

"I don't think Charlie Lane was a killer or ever could be without extreme provocation. If he didn't kill Hazel Franklin he didn't kill himself... Were there any prints on that automatic?"

"There never are any prints on a gun that are worth a damn."

"That isn't what I asked. Were there any prints of any kind?"

"No."

"No smudges?"

"No, damn it. The gun was clean as a whistle."

Murdock pulled his legs in and suddenly he felt a lot better.

"Then Charlie didn't pull the trigger."

Bacon seemed unimpressed.

"Didn't he?"

"It was an automatic. To get a shell in the chamber you have to pull back the slide. You have to push the clip home. You can't handle a gun, even with gloves, without leaving a smudge somewhere. If that automatic was clean someone else used it. Someone else put it close to his head and pulled the trigger."

Murdock took a quick breath as the excitement began to stir inside.

"Whoever did it wouldn't know you practically never get a decent print from a gun. To be sure he left no prints he probably wiped that automatic clean. Then, with the gun still in his handkerchief, he put it on the floor where you found it."

Bacon stopped teetering but nothing had changed in his face. That he made no argument was encouraging. After a pause he said:

"What else have you got that's interesting?"

"Charlie had a gun."

"How do you know?"

"He told me. Last year when he got that job at the motel. He was around there alone at night and sometimes there was quite a lot of money in the till. The owner thought it might be a good idea if there was a gun around, so Charlie got a permit. Chief Nickerson signed the application. You could check that permit. You could find out what kind of a gun—"

He stopped abruptly, held by some small change in the lieutenant's expression. Something that could have been the faintest of smiles had warped his lips. To anyone who did not know him that smile would have been unrecognizable. But when Murdock detected it he saw a gleam of interest in the gray eyes where none had been before. And suddenly he knew that he was right. More important, he understood that Bacon was 'way ahead of him and was merely letting him speak his piece before saying so.

"Damn you, Bacon," he said with some exasperation. "You've already checked it."

Sure.

"What kind of a gun did Charlie have?"

"A .38 R & R." Bacon snorted bruskly. "What do you think we are down here, stupes? You think we take everything for granted? Sure we checked for a permit."

"Charlie didn't kill himself."

"You could be right," Bacon said. "Not so much because a foreign automatic did the job—it's possible he picked it up somewhere but not likely; if he had suicide in mind he already had a gun of his own—but because there's only one way the gun could be so clean. The way you figured it."

He blew out his breath and his moment of condescension was over.

"We can't have a nice simple suicide," he said irritably. "We have to have a murder that hooks up with another murder and we ain't got much on that one either."

"You didn't find the .38?"

"No, but we found a box of shells for it in one of those suitcases."

"What about Darrow? Where was he around nine?"

"He had dinner with a guy. As near as we can tab it he left the restaurant around a quarter of nine. He walked home, so he says. It was a nice evening and he wanted the exercise. His wife says he got to the apartment between nine fifteen and nine twenty."

"How does that check out?" Murdock asked.

"It checks okay if he walked. But it's no more than seven or eight minutes from the restaurant to Lane's room. If he did the shooting he could have walked back to the Square, grabbed a cab, and made it home okay. He would have had time to spare."

Bacon fell silent and his chair was still. He was no longer looking at Murdock. His gray gaze was fixed straight ahead and there was distance in it now. When he finally spoke his blunt voice seemed softly reflective. "That Franklin dame really must have had something."

Because the remark was so unexpected Murdock did not understand it. He had to ask what Bacon meant.

"I had quite a talk with Mrs. Darrow. I can't figure a guy walking out on a woman like that."

"She's the one who went to Florida."

"Don't quibble," Bacon said. "That's a lot of woman. For my dough she's got everything—looks, figure, intelligence, the works. She's got dignity but you know damn well she's not one of those dames that gives you a lot of surface glamour and is all dried up and empty inside. This one has class, but if she was for you I'll bet she'd never push you out of bed on a cold night."

For Bacon, who had been married a long time and seldom had a flattering word for any woman, this was extravagant praise indeed. If his compliments were not poetically phrased they were at least convincing and left no doubt about his sentiments. Murdock waited, grinning a little at this seldom revealed facet of the lieutenant's personality and hoping for more. Presently the epilogue came.

"What did this Franklin woman have? From what I heard she was a greedy little bitch. What was she, a sex pot or something?"

"I don't think it was that," Murdock said. "She was just different. Mrs. Darrow is the statuesque, dark-haired type. Hazel was small and blonde. She wasn't married to Darrow and didn't have to put up with him as a steady diet. There was no background of domestic trouble, none of the friction that comes with marriage. Personally I think she was out for what she could get and she caught Darrow on the rebound and she was ready to use all the tricks in her bag."

He hesitated as he recalled the things Darrow had told him yesterday morning.

"I think Darrow was beginning to understand what she was like and wonder if he hadn't made a mistake. I think maybe he was getting ready to call it off, to realize that his wife was worth two Hazels."

"If you're right," Bacon said, "a situation like that could make a good motive. That Franklin woman could probably have made one hell of a lot of trouble."

"Where was Mrs. Darrow Saturday night?"

"She got to her apartment around six—we found the hack that brought her from the airport. She was too tired to go out to dinner and there was nothing but canned stuff in the kitchen, so she sent to a delicatessen about a block away for bread and butter and cold cuts and some salad. She made coffee and had supper alone. The delicatessen remembers the order."

"Then Darrow never was there."

"Hell, no. If he didn't have such a smart lawyer we might try pulling him in, but it probably wouldn't do much good. The D.A. says we got to get more before he makes his move. I've got a couple of men on him now."

"What about Herrick?"

"We know where he ate. We know he left at eight thirty. He says he was home after that and we can't prove he wasn't—not yet anyway."

Murdock considered telling the truth about last night, but not for long. To give details would be to run smack into a lengthy and difficult explanation of how he got those letters from Hazel Frankhn's apartment. He might still have to produce his two films but he certainly did not want to borrow trouble unnecessarily.

"Did you locate Hazel Franklin's brother?"

"Yeah. He's in town now. I sent him over to see that writer friend of yours—"

"Emerly?"

"—so he could get the story about that contract. We gave him a key to his sister's apartment."

"It's not sealed any more?"

"No." Bacon cocked one brow. "You want to shake the place down in case we missed something?"

"You didn't find anything there that would give you even a clue, hunh?"

"No. If you want to look around go ask the brother—his name is Leeman; he's probably going through her things now."

Murdock stood and pulled down his jacket and Bacon studied him a moment before he spoke.

"This Charlie Lane was a friend of yours, so you want to find out who killed him."

"I want to do what I can."

"Maybe you'll admit now that he knew who killed the woman and tried to cash in on it. He tried to put the bite on the wrong guy and got killed for it. He wouldn't tell you—or us."

Such a reminder was discouraging because Murdock had been trying not to think about that aspect of the case. Now, although forced to admit certain truths, he still defended his friend.

"It doesn't follow that he knew who the killer was."

"He knew something."

"Sure. Enough to embarrass somebody. If he knew the killer, if he was the kind of blackmailer you're trying to make him, he would have been more careful and set himself up for a big score... Two hundred and fifty bucks," he said bitterly. "That's all he wanted, and he probably would have settled for less. If he had collected he'd be on his way to Florida right now."

He walked to the door, turned back. "And the guy who did it didn't have guts enough to walk in and do the job and take his chances. He had to frame it and plant that jewelry—"

"Lane pawned that ring himself," Bacon cut in. "We got a description from the pawnbroker."

"All right. So he was given the ring and told to pawn it for part payment on the two fifty. He got one sixty and maybe he expected to get the difference last night. All that changes nothing. The killer came up alongside of him and pulled the trigger and hoped you'd fall for the suicide so Charlie would be blamed for killing Hazel Franklin. Well, whoever did it isn't going to get away with it, so you better keep punching before you get the *Courier* on your back."

Bacon took it in silence. He had seldom seen Murdock so worked up and he seemed to understand that further comment would be pointless. So he said nothing at all when Murdock opened the door and started out; neither did Murdock.

CHAPTER 19

MURDOCK HAD a bowl of soup and a sandwich for lunch and the time spent at the corner table away from the other customers was profitable because his mind worked uninterruptedly as he ate. He thought first of Hazel Franklin, considering the things Bacon had said as he reviewed his own understanding of her character. When he went on to consider Carl Darrow he suddenly remembered the detail that had thus far escaped him, and knew what he had to do about it.

Klime was alone in the anteroom of the studio when Murdock entered. He said things were quiet and Murdock said that was good and told him to take any calls that came in. He didn't want to be bothered and if anyone wanted him he would call back.

In the printing room he went immediately to the homemade file which was the receptacle for negatives the men had made. Fashioned of wood, it was a little higher than his head and perhaps three feet wide, a cabinet-like contrivance divided into compartments or pigeonholes. There were three main sections, each representing a month, and each section had thirty-one pigeonholes to indicate the days of the month. It was the job of the office boy to remove the oldest negatives each day, and the result was a three-month filing system that was always up-to-date.

The negatives Murdock wanted were filed under Sunday's date and he went through the pile until he found the two shots he had made of Hazel Franklin's body. Returning the others, he stepped to the enlarger, inserted a film, and raised the lens as far as he could. The light in the housing projected a picture on the white paper of the easel and he studied it in detail before he substituted the second negative.

Both showed a tiny object on the floor near the body. It would have taken a much bigger picture to make this object recognizable to one unfamiliar with the scene, but since Murdock already knew what it was he set about making the proper enlargement.

There was a seldom used device here for making outsized prints and he began his preparations by taking the enlarger from its standard and fastening it horizontally to another which had been made for that purpose. A white screen on a roller had been fastened to one wall and when Murdock pulled it down and secured it he had a makeshift easel. With one film still in the enlarger he adjusted the focus until the projection was clear. The bright object which had heretofore been tiny became a recognizable tieclip, and now he made faint marks on the screen so he would know its exact location.

With the light off in the enlarger, he took an eight by ten sheet of paper from the cabinet and cut it in half. He repeated the process several times because he knew he would have to experiment with the time of exposure. When he was ready he fastened a piece of sensitized paper to the proper spot in the screen with gummed tape, snapped on the light, and began to count... He watched the image take shape in the developing tank, examined it briefly, and tried again. When he found the third print satisfactory, he repeated the procedure with the second negative and then compared the two prints. The first seemed the better of the two so he made a duplicate before he rolled up the screen and restored the enlarger to its proper place.

Replacing the negatives in the filing cabinet, he left his prints in the tank and went back to his desk. The number he wanted came to mind as he lifted the telephone, and presently George Emerly's voice answered.

"George?" he said. "Murdock. Are you working?"

"Reading... Hey, I read in the paper about that guy Lane. Wasn't he the one you introduced me to down at Bayview?"

"He's the one."

"What the hell happened? Do you think it has anything to do with Hazel Franklin?"

"Could be."

"Well, I'll be damned." Emerly hesitated and said: "The account I read didn't say so but sort of gave the idea it might have been suicide."

"The police aren't saying—yet. But I think it was murder. That's why I called you. I think I've got a lead, George. It's nothing I can go to the police with now but if it works out maybe you could give me a hand."

"Sure, if I can."

"What I mean is," Murdock said, "I may want a witness. Where'll you be in—say another hour or so?"

"I'll be right here all afternoon."

"Fine, I'll call back if I can set it up."

Murdock went back to the printing room, rolled the excess liquid out of the best two photographs, and put them on the ferrotyper. The others he crumpled into a wet ball and threw it into the waste receptacle. He lit a cigarette while he waited and when the prints began to buckle with their drying he slipped them from the ferrotyper.

Because the light was not good here, he took them to his office for a closer examination and what he saw pleased him. The reproduction of the tie-clip was grainy, as he had expected, but it was well focused and distinct enough for his purpose, and he knew that an even more exact copy could be made if necessary. He took the gold tie-clip from his pocket and made a final comparison before he locked one of the prints in the center drawer; the duplicate and the clip were returned to his pocket.

Murdock had no intention of breaking into Hazel Franklin's apartment when he left the *Courier*. He expected to find her brother there, as Bacon had suggested, but when he could get no reply to his knocks he decided to enter the same way he entered on Saturday night, rather than delay the plan that was already working in his mind. He had no trouble finding what he wanted and he took a moment to notice that the brother had already been at work.

The closet was empty now. The dresses, some still in laundry bags, had been piled high on the bed and beside them were other piles of clothing. Shoes had been lined up on the floor, a wardrobe trunk, apparently brought up from the basement, stood open, as were the drawers of the chest and bureau. In all he was there no more than three minutes and when he reached the street he hailed a taxi and gave a riverside address.

The woman who opened the door in response to Murdock's ring was nearly as tall as he was, and the instant he saw Enid Darrow he recalled the comments Lieutenant Bacon had made. Clad in a navy woolen dress that was simply tailored and form-fitting but not tight, she had an erect, deep-breasted figure, dark-brown hair that held a hint of red, and greenish eyes, well spaced and slightly upward slanting at the corners. They seemed direct but expressionless as he introduced himself, and her voice had a soft throaty quality when she replied.

"If it's about my husband," she said, "I've already talked to the police and I have nothing further to say. Certainly nothing for publication."

"I didn't come as a reporter, Mrs. Darrow." Murdock hesitated, still held by her eyes and treading lightly. "What I want is a little more personal. It does concern your husband, and it could be important."

"Will it take long?"

"I shouldn't think so."

"Very well."

She stood aside and let him enter; then led the way into a spacious living room that overlooked the river and the Cambridge shore at one end. She sat down on the divan which faced the fireplace but she did not lean back when she asked him to sit down. She was still watching him, very cool and composed as she waited for him to state his case, and because Murdock sensed that the going would be difficult with a conventional approach he decided on a more unorthodox opening.

He smiled and said: "You said the police were here. Then you met Lieutenant Bacon... I talked with him around noon and he was very much impressed."

"Really?" she said, her tone suggesting she could not care less. "Favorably, I hope."

"Very," Murdock said, and took the plunge. "He couldn't understand how any man who had you for a wife could possibly see anything in Hazel Franklin." He went on quickly as she started to interrupt. "I said maybe it was because she was so different. I said there could have been trouble between you and your husband; I mean the domestic kind, friction of one sort or another that led to mis understandings. All Hazel had to do was use her wits and make sure the things she did were what your husband wanted most."

"Wasn't that rather presumptuous?"

"I beg your pardon."

"Why should you say anything at all? You don't even know me."

"But I had seen you. And I did know Hazel. For several years. Not well, but enough to know what she was like. I also know your husband and I found myself agreeing with the lieutenant. I still don't know what Hazel could do for him that you couldn't do better, assuming that you cared enough to try."

He saw her expression change as he finished. In the beginning she had been reserved and a little annoyed, but he had her interest now. This was the subject that was closest to her and when her eyes moved on it seemed to him that the things they saw were in her mind and had no part of the room.

"Yes," she said. "One has to care enough to try."

"You didn't get the divorce you went for, did you?"

"No."

"Then you must have cared more than you thought."

"I always did care but it was not that simple... Friction? Certainly there was friction. I thought Carl should spend just a little more time with me and less with his business affairs. I wanted children, or at least one child, before it was too late, but he could not forget that he had served a sentence for manslaughter. He said it wouldn't be fair to a child to have a father with such a record. He said the past would keep cropping up to haunt him.

"I don't believe that," she said, her eyes coming back to Murdock now but the look in them suggesting she was no longer aware that he was a stranger. He was, at the moment, simply a sympathetic but objective target for the thoughts and feelings that had become so important to her.

"Why does he have to live here?" she demanded. "An assistant could take care of this end of his business. We could live any number of places that are more pleasant than this. It would be better for us to make new friends, better for a child who was growing up."

She paused again and Murdock was afraid to say anything lest he break the mood of her confession. He did not move a muscle or make a sound until she continued. "I knew he loved me," she said, "and I thought I had that hold over him that every woman seems to think she has over a man. He wanted the warmth and affection he knew was part of my nature and he got silence and indifference, the distant manner, the dignified response. It was nothing a man would want to come home to and he had the money and the good looks to do something about it.

"I don't know when he first started seeing Hazel but I found out about it soon enough, and when I finished delivering my ultimatum I had very little left but my pride. I went to Florida and the longer I stayed the more I realized what a fool I was. Maybe it was pride that brought me back, maybe it was the certain knowledge that I still loved him and the hope that he could love me if he had the chance. Whatever the reason I knew I could not let anyone as cheap and grasping as Hazel Franklin have him by default. That's why I came home and—"

She broke off suddenly, her color high and a new gleam in the green eyes. One minute she was intent only on voicing the things that had been bottled up inside her for too long; the next she became aware of the circumstances and was annoyed with herself for being so forthright with her confidence. He could see the change as her shoulders straightened and her mouth compressed.

"You wanted to talk about my husband," she said. "You said it might be important. Just what did you mean by that?"

Murdock knew the interview was over and he rose and moved closer to her. He took the tie-clip from his pocket and placed it on his palm so she could get a good look at it.

"Do you recognize this, Mrs. Darrow?"

"Why"—she took one look and when her glance came up it held a look of puzzlement—"yes. I gave it to him last Christmas. It was part of a set."

"The cuff links have blue stones in the center?"

"Small sapphires." She rose and glanced again at the clip. "Where did you get it?"

"I found it."

"Well—" She smiled then, her manner suddenly gracious. "Thank you. I'll give it to him when—"

Murdock cut her off, not liking the. idea but having no choice.

"I'd rather give it to him myself, Mrs. Darrow," he said.

"You can tell him I have it. Tell him I found it Saturday night."

He backed toward the foyer. He offered a small nod and a perfunctory smile as he thanked her for seeing him.

She was still watching wide-eyed and unmoving when he turned and headed for the door.

CHAPTER 20

AS SOON AS Murdock reached the street he headed for a drugstore a block and a half away. In the telephone booth he dialed Jack Fenner's number and felt a small thrust of relief when the detective answered.

"What did you find out about Paul Herrick?"

"Not much, chum. Not much."

"For instance?"

"I got nowhere on the bank end. Your pal Bacon could tell you about that, couldn't he? Or aren't you confiding in him these days?"

"Well what did you get?"

"This engagement he's starting next week at the Melody Grill. It's a quartet, right? He collects nine hundred, so how much would that be for him?"

"Probably four or maybe four fifty."

"He hit the boss for a six hundred cash advance on Friday. That's about all I've got so far. I could keep working on it if you—"

"Never mind ... I'd rather you did something else," Murdock said, and then he was explaining what he had in mind. This time Fenner was doubtful.

"I don't know," he said. "If I get caught on a thing like that I could lose my license."

"Not if you do it my way."

Fenner listened and then gave his grudging approval.

"You're thinking pretty good today. Okay. I'll see you when I finish. That should just about use up the eight hours you're paying me for."

Murdock went back to the *Courier* and rode to the fifth floor. He found the entertainment editor in his little cubby, but the information he got did no more than corroborate what he had already learned from Jack

Fenner, so he continued on to the city room to speak to the man at the desk.

"I'll be at my place if anyone wants me," he said. "I probably won't be back."

"Sure," the editor said. "We can handle things from here." He picked up a telephone, dialed once. "Hello," he said. "Who's this?" He covered the mouthpiece with his palm. "Delaney's there now."

"I'll speak to him before I leave," Murdock said.

In the studio he told Delaney what he had told the city editor and then went into his little office and closed the door before he called George Emerly.

"How about it, George?" he said. "Still interested?"

"Sure," Emerly said. "But can you fill me in a little? Do you really think you know who killed Hazel?"

"It's only a hunch so far," Murdock said, "but I think we can work it out. It's worth a try anyway. The only thing is, it may get a little rough if I'm right."

"Oh?"

"I think I can prove that Carl Darrow was at the Pine Grove Motel Saturday night. I think he was the one who drove Hazel there and then disappeared. I had a talk with his wife and I have an idea he'll be paying me a call. He was a pretty tough guy once; he may still be."

"Yes, but—he certainly won't talk in front of me."

"Not in front of you, George," Murdock said. "If you get there first he's not going to know you're there at all."

"I get it... Sure," Emerly said. "When do you want me?"

"Soon. I'm at the office but I'll be home in about five minutes. Come when you're ready and remember what I said. Darrow could get rough."

Kent Murdock was still thinking hard when he unlocked the door of his apartment a few minutes later and stepped inside. He closed the door, pocketed the key, and turned round before he saw Paul Herrick watching him from the wing chair near one of the two windows that overlooked the street.

In that first moment or two neither moved. Murdock swallowed his surprise and stood where he was, his dark gaze narrowing as it focused on the gun Herrick held. It was not so much the gun that started the tension working on him—it looked like his own automatic—what bothered him most was the expression on the big man's face. He wore loafers and a pair of gray flannel slacks and a rumpled tweed jacket with leather patches at the elbows. His tie was askew and the collar unbuttoned. The handsome features seemed shiny, the brows were bunched, and the light-brown eyes held a look of harassment and frustration. Now, as he came slowly out of the chair and leveled the gun, Murdock said:

"You must be nuts."

"Yeah," said Herrick. "Ever since Saturday night. And it's getting worse, Murdock. It's getting so I just don't give a damn. I've been working here for two hours."

He gestured with the gun. "Out there in that darkroom of yours. I went through every goddamned film you had in those files and it isn't there. So now I'm going over this place inch by inch and you're going to help—unless you want to make it easy on yourself. Get me those two films you made from my letters and I'll take off."

Murdock let his breath out slowly and flexed his fingers. In his present mood Herrick was dangerous and Murdock knew it. The big hand was tight on the gun but it was a shaky hand now. The nerves that controlled it were ragged and uncertain and in such a condition the pressure on the trigger could easily get too great. The thought scared Murdock because he understood that Herrick was no longer quite rational on the subject of the letters he had once written; in his mind they still threatened his coming marriage and future happiness. He had already lived with that thought too long, and because Murdock knew that to cross him now would be foolish, he tipped one hand and tried to keep the concern from his voice.

"What do you expect to prove with that gun?" he asked finally.

"That depends." Herrick moved the muzzle. "It's your gun, Murdock. If it should go off real close who is going to tie me in with the job?"

"That would be kind of silly."

"Maybe. I'm just telling you what could happen if you get cute. Why can't you get it through that thick head that all I want is those negatives. If you're going to be stubborn about it I can always use it to club you with, but right now we're going to start looking." He jerked the gun toward the desk.

"Start there. Take any drawer and empty it on the floor one piece at a time. I'm going to stand right here and watch and when we finish with the desk—"

The sound of the buzzer cut him off and without moving, his body seemed to recoil. He glanced at the door, his hand unconsciously tightening on the gun. He looked back at Murdock, the wild glints still in his eyes and white spots showing through the tan at his cheekbones.

"Stay quiet," he warned. "We'll wait."

Murdock had no time to feel relief. He had one eye on the gun and the stiffness was still in back of his neck.

"It won't do any good," he said quietly.

"What the hell do you mean?"

"He knows I'm here. He'll keep buzzing until I answer the door."

"Who?"

"George Emerly."

"The writer?"

Murdock nodded and Herrick made up his mind. He took a new grip on the automatic and his brows came down.

"All right," he said softly, as the buzzer sounded again. "It's not going to make any difference now. Open it," he said. "I'll be right behind you."

He moved up as Murdock started for the door, and now the pressure of the gun was in his back. He turned the knob, pulled carefully. When he saw Emerly he winked and tried to signal with a small jerk of his head. He began to back up, aware that Herrick had stepped out of the way. Then, seeing the startled look in Emerly's eyes, he knew that he too had seen the gun.

"Come in," Herrick said. "Close the door."

Emerly obeyed, an odd stiffness in his tall, lanky frame, a hard bright glint in his bespectacled eyes as he addressed Murdock.

"What kind of a deal is this?" he asked curtly. "You told me over the phone that—"

"I know what I told you," Murdock interrupted. "And that's how it was supposed to be. This is new. Herrick was waiting with the gun when I came in. He wants to search the place."

"Skip the details." Herrick indicated the divan. "Sit down over there, Emerly. Stay there and behave." He waited until Emerly eased down on the cushions and then looked at Murdock. "Get started," he said. "The middle drawer first."

Murdock sat down at the desk and pulled out the drawer. He placed it on the top. He picked out a handful of bills and receipts and fanned them out so Herrick could see them. As he bent over to put them on the floor he saw that the other stood five feet away, no longer pointing the automatic but holding it in readiness. He took a handful of letters and began to sort them and then Emerly's voice cut through the silence, harsh and incisive.

"Stand still, Herrick! Don't lift your hand."

Murdock was watching Herrick when it happened. He saw the big man stiffen and his head jerk round. There was that instant of startled indecision and then it was too late because Herrick's left side was toward Emerly and it was the right hand which held the automatic.

"Good," Emerly said, his voice still tight. "Now drop the gun."

Murdock forced his glance beyond Herrick. Emerly was leaning across the arm of the divan. The short-barreled revolver in his hand was pointed right at Herrick, and even as he looked at Emerly, Murdock heard the automatic thud to the rug somewhere behind him.

"All right," Emerly said. "Step back. Do you want to get it, Kent?"

Murdock rose and retrieved his gun. When he examined it he saw that no bullet had been jacked into the chamber and he left it that way before he slipped it into his hip pocket. Emerly stood up and shoved his gun down inside his belt.

"Now what?" he said. "What the hell's the matter with this guy anyway?" he added with a glance at Herrick.

Murdock made no reply. He could feel the tension ease inside, but the perspiration was trickling down his sides and he found he had lost some of the enthusiasm for the plan he had visualized. If this much could go wrong in the very beginning there was no telling what might happen, and for the first time he realized he might be getting in over his head.

A glance at Herrick told him the big man no longer presented much of a problem. He had not moved but the broad shoulders had sagged and his eyes had the whipped and beaten look of a man who had lost all hope. The handsome face was slack and shiny and bewildered, as though he was just now beginning to understand how far out on the limb he had gone in his irrational efforts to get back his letters. He stood mute and immobile as Murdock started for the telephone.

When the man at police headquarters informed him that Lieutenant Bacon was not in, Murdock swore softly. Because he had no alternative now, he left a message.

"Tell him Murdock has been trying to get him. Tell him to get in touch with me... That's right... I'll be at my place. Yeah."

He hung up and faced Herrick. "You knew Hazel was going to be at the motel Saturday."

"Yes, I knew. She was supposed to call me at the club when she got in."

"Why?"

Herrick took a breath and let it out noisily. He glanced round for a chair, found one, and sat down.

"I was supposed to buy the letters back."

"You'd already been paying her a hundred a week."

"Sure. But she knew I was getting married and she thought once that happened she was through collecting. She said I could have them for two thousand cash. By borrowing and cleaning out my bank account and getting an advance on the Melody Grill job I raised it."

Murdock spun the desk chair about and sat down. "Did she call you?"

"Yes. About ten after eight. I was eating dinner. She said she'd talk to me later. When she didn't show up I got worried and ducked over to the motel."

"That was when I saw you driving out, wasn't it? What did you do? What did she say?"

"I didn't see her. The lights were on and the radio was playing but nobody answered my knock." He swallowed, a note of desperation in his voice. "That's the truth. Honest to God."

"I believe you," Murdock said. "If you knew she was dead at nine thirty you sure as hell wouldn't have gone back to the club. You'd have high-tailed it for town and her apartment to look for those letters. So you went back around eleven thirty or so. After you'd talked to Darrow."

"I thought she'd come down with him but Carl said no. He said he'd been in town all evening." Herrick hesitated and wet his lips. "So I told my guitar player to take over the piano and went back to the motel. When there still was no answer to my knock I looked through the Venetian blinds. By standing on tiptoe I could just see her."

Murdock remembered how he had almost been able to see the object on the floor between the beds, remembered thinking that if he were taller or had something to stand on he could have made sure. And Herrick was taller and—

"She didn't move," the big man said, cutting in on his thoughts, "and I knew she wasn't drunk because she never would take more than two drinks. I wasn't sure she was dead but I knew what I had to do and I got in the car and started for her apartment. I was still there when you walked in."

Murdock glanced at Emerly and then back at Herrick.

What he had heard sounded convincing and he wanted to believe it because it seemed to fit with the theory he had formed. He might have said so if the drone of the buzzer had not filled the room and reminded him of other things. He moved quickly then, turning Herrick toward the bedroom door and motioning to Emerly to follow.

"In there," he whispered. "Get behind the door and stay quiet until I tell you to come out."

Herrick's eyes opened, so did his mouth. He seemed about to protest but there was an urgency in Murdock's words, and the gesture that Emerly made silenced him. The two disappeared as the buzzer sounded again and Murdock straightened the desk and replaced the drawer before he stepped up to open the door.

Carl Darrow entered slowly after Murdock had stepped aside. He wore an expensive-looking but loose-fitting gabardine topcoat and beneath the brown felt his tanned, boxlike face was inscrutable, the black eyes prying and intent as they slid past Murdock to inspect the room. He said nothing at all as he closed the door with one elbow and he kept moving, to the center of the room first, then toward the bedroom. He did not enter but gave the interior a quick glance from a distance of five feet, turned and went on to look into the kitchen. When he came back he went to the windows and looked down on the street below for a second or two before sitting down in the wing chair. During all this time his hands had not moved from his coat pockets and they remained there as he spoke.

"I hear you've got something that belongs to me. A tieclip, wasn't it?"

Murdock lit a cigarette and sat down at the desk. "That's right," he said, when he had inhaled.

"Why did you bother my wife?"

"I wanted to find out whether it was yours."

"You could have asked me."

"I like it better this way," Murdock said. "I'd rather talk here than in your office with that driver of yours hanging around. What's his name?"

"Leslie." Darrow lowered his chin and studied Murdock from beneath the hat brim. "You found it Saturday night, hunh? Where?"

"Haven't you any idea where you lost it?"

"If I had I wouldn't be asking."

"Beside Hazel's body," Murdock said, and then he was relating the details as he remembered them. "It looks something like my clip," he said. "Gold and about the same shape. If I had taken a good look at it I would have known it wasn't mine. But I didn't. I was thinking of too many other things and when Charlie asked me and I saw my own clip was missing I said it was mine."

He went on to tell what had happened to his own clip and how it had been returned to him by Lucille Dunn. "If I'd known about it Sunday I probably would have given it to Chief Nickerson or that state police lieutenant."

"But you didn't."

"You know I didn't."

"So what're you driving at?"

"I'm saying you were with Hazel Franklin in that motel room. You probably drove her there. I can't prove that— yet. I can't prove you killed her but I can prove you

knew she was dead before you tried to use Lucille and fix
up an alibi."

"I haven't heard any proof yet." Darrow's husky voice
was low, even, and menacing, but nothing had changed in
his face. "You say you found my clip there. I say you
didn't. The only one who could prove you're right is that
caddy, Charlie Lane—and he's dead."

"I can do a little better than that."

Murdock rose and took the four by five print from his
pocket. He looked at it a moment before he stepped over
to hand it to Darrow.

"When Charlie and I found the body," he said, "I took
two pictures. The clip was on the floor. This is a blowup of
that clip taken from the original negative. It's pretty good
now but it can be made better."

Darrow studied the print in silence, only the top of
his hat visible from where Murdock stood. His right hand
was still deep in his topcoat pocket and when he finally
tipped his head his narrowed gaze was suspicious.

"You can have that," Murdock said. "There are other
copies."

"How come you didn't turn this in to the cops?"

"I called Bacon a while ago. He wasn't in."

Darrow slipped the print into his pocket. "I knew I
lost it," he said, half to himself. "I wasn't sure where." He
hesitated. When he spoke again his jaw was hard and his
eyes were half closed.

"I did some time for manslaughter," he said. "I was
guilty, so I didn't have much of a beef. It could have been
called self-defense but the D.A. thought I'd been a bad
boy and the manslaughter rap stuck. This is a little
different, Murdock. I don't know why you stuck your nose
in. I asked you the other day if you were playing detective
and you said no."

"I wasn't—then. I said I didn't care too much who
killed Hazel. But I liked Charlie Lane. I know now he
must have got a little out of line but there was nothing
mean or vicious about him and if he'd got the small

payment he wanted he would never have bothered anyone. I resent like hell the cowardly way he was killed and I promised myself to do something about it if I could. Now I think I can. That's why I'm crowding you. You've got a chance to talk to me if you want to before you talk to Bacon but if you think I'm just making a speech you can pull your sox up and beat it."

Darrow listened without interruption. He may even have been impressed. His lips moved and were still and he gave a small nod before he spoke.

"I like it here," he said. "What's the rush? Why shouldn't I talk to you, you're not going anywhere... Yeah, I was there Saturday night," he said. "I drove her down. I didn't figure to spend the night—not there anyway—but I thought we'd have dinner at the club. I was figuring on the right way to get rid of her, if you want to know the truth. I'd begun to compare her with my wife and she wasn't even in the same league. I thought it might cost me because Hazel always had her little hand out, but I wasn't worried too much."

He coughed and said: "She registered and gave a phony license number like I told her to do. We went in with the bags and then I remembered I didn't have any whisky. I didn't even take off my hat. I went back to the car and drove to town—you know how far it is—and picked up a bottle and drove right back. I was gone maybe fifteen minutes."

"What time would that be?"

"About twenty after eight when I walked in on her."

"Okay." Murdock turned his head slightly and called to the bedroom. "George."

There was no reaction from Darrow until he saw Emerly appear in the doorway with Herrick behind him. Then he jerked erect in the chair and his hand moved in his pocket.

Understanding came quickly as he looked back at Murdock.

"Why you miserable bastard!"

Murdock met the infuriated stare with steady eyes and mentally crossed his fingers. When Darrow made no other move he glanced at Emerly who looked scared but kept coming. Finally he nodded to Herrick.

"Look between the mattress and spring, Paul," he said.

"What?"

"The films you want are in the bed."

A look of utter disbelief crossed Herrick's face and his jaw sagged. It took him another second or two to understand Murdock's meaning and then he spun about and practically dived through the bedroom door. Murdock could hear the squeak of the bed as the mattress was thrown aside and then Herrick was back, still staring in wonderment at the two negatives.

"I don't get it," he said finally.

"I had to be sure about the time," Murdock said. "You were eating dinner between seven thirty and eight thirty Saturday night. It's an alibi that stands up now and those films no longer matter. Why don't you take them with you and we can both forget them."

Herrick's features seemed to dissolve as realization came to him. He seemed so overwhelmed with gratitude that Murdock was afraid he might break into tears, so he moved up and touched his arm to steer him toward the door. Herrick was still looking down at the negatives as he went out. In the hall he turned and tried to say something but the words seemed to stick in his throat and Murdock helped him out.

"Forget it," he said, and waited until Herrick reached the stairs before he closed the door.

CHAPTER 21

CARL DARROW was still in the chair and Emerly was eying him warily, his jacket open and his hand inside, apparently on the butt of his revolver. Murdock sat down on the arm of the divan and Darrow said:

"What the hell was that all about?"

"Hazel was blackmailing him," Murdock said. "He was a pretty fair suspect until you just cleared him."

"So," Darrow said. "I cleared him, hunh?"

"Before a witness," Murdock said and nodded toward Emerly. "You took Hazel to the motel and your tie-clip was found beside her body That much we know."

"It's not enough," Darrow said, "because my story is that she was on the floor when I came back with the liquor. I didn't know what was the matter with her and I dropped down beside her and lifted her to a sitting position before I saw the stocking and guessed what had happened, That tie-clip must have caught in her slip, or one of the shoulder straps."

"You got out in a hurry."

"You're damn right I got out in a hurry. People knew I'd been running around with her. They could prove I'd given her presents. I might even have dropped the word that I was going to break it up. The D.A. could make it look like she wouldn't go for that, that we got in a row and I blew my top and grabbed her."

He said: "I got out of there and I wanted an alibi and I thought of the little blonde who'd been pestering me for a job in Florida and a chance to sing. She was perfect for what I wanted and I was lucky because she'd just come back to her cottage and she was dressed and she was alone. I don't even think anyone saw me because I left my car by the side of the road and cut up the slope on the far

side where her room was. I told her I needed an alibi and
if she wanted that Florida spot she'd better come along.
"When we got in the car I told her we were going to have
dinner in town, that she was to say she'd been with me all
evening. It would have been okay except for that accident
that held me up and the pictures you took. Maybe it was
a bad idea but at the time I was afraid my license number
would show and spoil everything. I had to make a choice
so I cued her and gave her some lines. She played them
okay too, but she only got two of those films."

The third was in my pocket," Murdock said. "She
never had a chance at it."

He hesitated, worried about what came next; then,
for the third time, the buzzer saved him and he moved
quickly, welcoming the interruption and finding the
sound a happy one because he had been waiting for it.

Jack Fenner was about Murdock's age, a wiry,
competent-looking man with straight black hair that was
receding and lay flat against his skull, and shrewd agate
eyes that were seldom still. Now, as Murdock opened the
door, he saw one eye wink deliberately and knew that
Fenner had completed his assignment.

"Come in," he said. "Do you know Carl Darrow and
George Emerly?"

Fenner nodded. "Hi, Carl."

"Hello, Jack."

"Mr. Emerly?"

Emerly said hello and Murdock glanced back at
Fenner.

"Do you want to sit in, Jack?" he said.

"Sure." Fenner went over and perched on a window
sill.

"Deal me a hand and I'll check the action."

Darrow had watched all this in silence, his muscular
face grim, his gaze again suspicious.

"Where do you fit?"

"I don't," Fenner said. "I'm just running errands for
Murdock—for a fee."

He produced a folded sheet of paper from an inside pocket and took a small leather case from a second pocket. He handed both to Murdock and sat back, folding his arms. Darrow cleared his throat. "I don't know what this is all about yet but I'm not going to sit still for any frame, Murdock."

"There doesn't have to be a frame but I had to get the time element worked out."

He sat down and leaned forward, forearms on his knees and hands dangling.

"Once we knew that jewelry had been planted on Charlie Lane," he said, "and that Hazel hadn't been killed by some prowler, there were only three of you in the picture. You, Herrick, and George."

"Me?" Emerly's eyes opened behind the glasses. "You're kidding."

"Not exactly." Murdock glanced at Darrow. "You cleared Herrick."

"So you say."

"And that leaves you and—"

"I didn't kill her—or Lane either for that matter."

"No," Murdock said, "I don't think you did." He looked at Emerly. "That was sort of a silly move, trying to get into Lucille Dunn's room last night. When I began to think about that, a lot of other things seemed to fall in place."

"What the devil are you talking about?" Emerly said.

Murdock repeated the story the girl had told him. When he finished he said: "It wouldn't make much sense for Carl or Paul to sneak into that room. She knew them both. She wasn't afraid of them. All they had to do was knock and she would have let them in. It was different with you. You couldn't be sure about her and there wasn't any light showing under the door—"

"I don't know what you're talking about," Emerly said.

"Okay." Murdock took a breath and tried to put his thoughts in order. He had a lot of things to say, no one of which seemed terribly important except as part of an overall pattern. He was not sure just where to start but he knew he had to try. "This may take a while," he said. "So bear with me."

He unfolded the sheet Fenner had given him, compared it with a similar sheet he had taken from Hazel Franklin's desk earlier in the afternoon.

"Jack just came from your place," he said with a nod toward Fenner. "I told him to wait until you came out before he tried to get in so he wouldn't get caught. One of the things I wanted was your copy of the contract you had with Hazel. This is it. This"—he held up the other sheet—"is her copy. If my idea is right, they're phonies."

"What idea?"

"An idea based on Hazel's character. Everyone who knew her—you, Darrow, Herrick, and Mrs. Darrow—used one or two words in describing her. Greedy. Grasping. She made you kick in with half the money you'd collected on Ted Franklin's old stories and I don't think she'd sign any contract that cut her share down to twenty-five per cent." He rose as he spoke and stepped to the window. The sky was still bright and he superimposed one copy of the contract over the other as he placed them against the glass so the light would shine through. The signatures stood out clearly. Until that moment he had been guessing about this element of his theory; now he knew he was right.

"Hazel didn't sign these," he said. "The signatures are identical in every respect. They'll tell you down at headquarters—and a handwriting man will confirm it— that nobody ever signs his name exactly the same way. You traced these, or copied them from some other signature, probably from one of the checks of yours she endorsed."

"Wait a minute." Darrow spoke bruskly. "What the hell is all this?"

"It's a long story."

"I got time. You got me here and I might as well hear the rest of it."

Murdock sighed and sat down again. He spoke of Ted Franklin's unsold stories and outlined the details that Emerly had given him on Saturday night and repeated again to Lieutenant Bacon.

"I believed you," he said to Emerly. "I think Bacon did too. You made it sound pretty convincing, but when I got to thinking about you I saw one thing wrong. You said Hazel recognized one of her husband's old stories, and came to collect a share of that and others you had used. You paid her. You've got cancelled checks to prove it. Why should you do that unless she could prove the original stories were Franklin's?"

He had Emerly's interest now. The long face was very grave but things were happening behind the bespectacled eyes and his voice was oddly quiet as he spoke.

"What do you mean, prove?"

"Unless she could back up her charge that you'd plagiarized those ideas she had no case against you. She couldn't go to court and say you stole a story just because she happened to remember copying a similar story for her husband. She would have to back up such a charge with evidence a court would recognize, and I think she had it or you wouldn't have paid her a dime. I think she had the originals of those old stories, the first drafts from which she had once typed the clean copies. For some reason— it's not important now—she must have kept those rough drafts. It's the only possible way she could prove her story, and you knew it."

He took a breath and said: "Bacon said he went over her apartment with a fine-tooth comb. He said there was nothing there that helped or pointed the finger at anyone. If those rough copies had been there he would have mentioned it because it's his business to be suspicious and he'd heard your side of the contract business. A man like Bacon, if he had those roughs, would have checked back. So I say there were no scripts in her apartment when the police got there. I also say there had to be scripts or she couldn't have collected from you. You took them Saturday night, didn't you?"

He hesitated, not expecting an answer, and then said:

"I looked in her closet when I was there that night. The front had been torn out of a laundry bag; you know, one of those long ones the dry cleaners use. I think you used that to wrap those scripts. You had to wrap them in something because if anyone happened to see you he'd remember a guy with an armful of typescript. I didn't ask Jack to look for them but I wouldn't be surprised if you still have them around somewhere, maybe down cellar where you keep trunks and things you're not using."

"You've got it all figured out, haven't you?" Emerly said in the same quiet tone.

"I'm trying," Murdock said.

"So let's get to the part where I killed her."

"I'll have to do some more guessing."

"Go ahead. Darrow says he's got plenty of time and Fenner's working for you. Start with the motive."

Murdock looked back at Emerly, a little discouraged now but aware that he had to keep pitching. He had not expected a voluntary confession but he still had some bits and pieces that might do the job one way or another.

"All right, George," he said. "Try this for size. You were paying Hazel fifty per cent of the stories you had used and sold, but I think you must have held out on one, probably the one you spoke of that brought a TV and a movie sale. I think she found out and you couldn't pay and she crowded you too far. If she had those old originals—and I still say she must have had them—she could have sued you, the magazine, the network, and the movie company. Not only could she have collected but she would have finished you as a writer. Once the truth came out you could never sell another line, not even to a newspaper.

"She had you over a barrel and she must have threatened you in some way or asked for terms that were impossible— or seemed so to you. Whatever the reason you decided to take the big gamble. I don't know whether you planned to kill her at the motel or not, but you must have considered the possibility; neither do I know whether you faked those contracts before you went down there or after you went back to her apartment. I don't see that it matters. What is important is that you must have known where she was going Saturday night and probably with whom. Maybe you went there ahead of time in the hope of getting her alone for a few minutes; maybe you followed Darrow's car. However you planned it, you were there when Darrow went out for the whisky. You walked in on her and it didn't take long."

He paused to see if there would be any reaction from Emerly. When none came he said: "You had luck all the way except for two things. Charlie Lane saw you somewhere around the grounds. So did Lucille Dunn, though she didn't realize it or even remember you. I phoned you at seven thirty Saturday night and the line was busy. I accepted that as proof that you were home talking to someone else, and I was wrong about that too. You simply left the phone off the hook. The busy signal gave you a superficial alibi but it won't stand up now. My man at the studio called later to give you the golf message. That was about ten o'clock and you answered, but you still had time to get to Hazel's, grab the scripts, and plant the phony agreement."

"That sounds pretty good," Emerly said. "If you could only back up the theory—"

"Hazel had no keys in her handbag. You took them because a key to her apartment was the one thing you had to have." Murdock brought out the ostrich-leather key case that Fenner had given him. "Where'd you find them, Jack?"

"In the back of a desk drawer."

"That's item number one," Murdock said. "I guess the police can prove the case was Hazel's... Item number two is a girl named Lucille Dunn... You can get her back here, can't you?" he said to Darrow.

"Item number three," Murdock said when Darrow nodded, "is the gun you've got in your belt."

"This one?"

Emerly moved as he spoke and the revolver was in his hand. The thin face held a grayish tinge now and suddenly the eyes mirrored a new brightness that seemed both panic-ridden and dangerous.

"That was quite a pitch you made to me over the telephone," he said, his tone shrill. "You needed help. You knew who killed Hazel and wanted a witness. Things might get very tough, you said. You wanted to scare me. You wanted me to bring the gun."

"I hoped you would," Murdock said.

"And suppose I use it?"

"That was a chance I had to take. That's why I wanted Darrow and Fenner around to give me some backing."

He watched the gun level at him as he finished and he let his breath out slowly. Because he was thinking now of Charlie Lane the feeling that came over him was basically one of satisfaction rather than alarm. He had worked hard for this moment, knowing that there would be some risk, aware that there was still a risk, not only to him but to everyone in the room.

"That's a .38 R & R, isn't it, George? Charlie's gun. You didn't know he had it when you went there last night, did you? You took a German gun that couldn't be traced and after you had used it you planted the ring and the watch in his bag. That's when you saw his gun and knew you had to take it with you to make the suicide idea hold water."

He paused, waiting for some reply. When none came he spoke softly and started to rise.

"That's all I've got, George. I think it's enough but let's let the district attorney decide about that."

He was moving slowly toward the telephone when Emerly stopped him. "Maybe it's a little late for that," he said. "Sit down. Over here." He jerked the gun toward the divan, watching Murdock obey as he backed to the desk chair and sat down to face the room.

CHAPTER 22

FOR SEVERAL SECONDS then there was no sound but the muted hum of traffic on the street outside. Jack Fenner's agate eyes were fixed on Emerly. Darrow had not moved, but his right hand was still in his pocket and the hat brim put his eyes in shadow and left his steady gaze obscure.

Murdock looked from one to the other and back at the gun in Emerly's hand. He tried to weigh the individual reactions and the odds, and at the moment he found them discouraging. He had set this up more or less according to plan and he was responsible for what happened now. He was sure that Darrow had a gun. In the beginning he had not been sure about Fenner because the detective did not always carry one. Now, seeing Fenner carelessly unbutton his jacket so it hung loose, he knew the score. It was Fenner who finally broke the silence.

"What do you think you're going to do with that?"

Emerly knew what he meant. He glanced at the revolver and readjusted his grip.

"I don't know."

"Maybe you'd better make up your mind."

"Why should I?"

"You're making me nervous." Fenner's statement was a lie and Murdock knew it. "If you're figuring on using it you'll only get one shot."

Emerly hesitated, his harried gaze on the move. "How do you figure that?"

"Carl's got a gun in his pocket. I've got one five inches from my right hand. I'm betting we're better than you are."

Emerly spoke to Darrow but no longer dared eye him directly. "Take it out of your pocket."

"I like it this way," Darrow said.

Murdock spoke quickly because he could feel the mounting pressure in the room and was afraid it might erupt in violence. To get Emerly's mind off the immediate problem and give Fenner and Darrow a chance to think things out, he said:

"How close was I, George?"

"Close enough."

Emerly swallowed visibly, his Adam's apple bobbing in his throat. The long face was shiny now and something else had happened to his eyes. There was fear of a kind but no viciousness, and when he spoke his voice sounded remote, resigned, and quite hopeless.

"You got one thing wrong," he said. "I don't expect you to understand but I have to tell you. It wasn't that story I sold to TV and the movies. That was mine. An original, just like I said. The first I ever wrote that really paid off... It was the book," he said.

"Oh," Murdock said. "So that was Franklin's too."

"He really never finished it, although he had a copy made. He couldn't seem to get the ending right and by then he was too discouraged by all the other rejects he'd had to care much. About that time the magazine assignment came along and he never mentioned it to me after that.

"I did a complete re-write," he said. "I spent a long time finishing it, but in the end it was worth it. If you're not a writer you wouldn't understand what it could mean to have it accepted, to know that you'd done something that would have a little permanence, that something of yours would stand on library shelves and maybe be translated and read all over the world. I knew Hazel would find out about it and I kept trying to get her to sign some sort of an agreement, but she was a suspicious woman and she kept putting me off."

He hesitated and said: "Last week she found out. I had page proofs in the filing cabinet—they'd been there quite a while—and she stopped by to pick up some work

I'd been doing. I went out to the kitchen to make some coffee and she got to snooping and found the proofs. She stuck them in her handbag and went home and read them and then she knew what I'd done because she had kept the first drafts, just like you said.

"We had it out Saturday afternoon," he said. "I couldn't argue with her. She wouldn't even listen to reason. I offered to pay her half of the advance that I'd already spent and half of everything that came in. I finally offered her seventy-five per cent because it was worth it to me just to have the book come out with my name on it. She said no. Not unless the book was published with Ted as co-author."

He hesitated again, his face twisted with his effort to make his listeners understand and believe him.

"How could they do that?" he asked. "Copies had already been printed. They were in the hands of the dealers and the reviewers. If they tried to call them back the story would come out and everybody'd know what I'd done... It didn't make any difference to her," he said, the bitterness underriding his words. "It was her way or nothing. I guess that's when I made up my mind. I knew about the weekend she'd planned and—"

He broke off, sighed, and shifted the gun. "What difference does it make?" he said. "You had it figured close enough. The details aren't important. I didn't try to frame anybody then. I knew you'd be coming back to find her"— he glanced at Darrow—"and maybe that's why I took the jewelry. I thought if the police started looking for a prowler I'd be safe enough."

"When did Charlie see you?"

"He saw me walking away from the place. He didn't actually see me come out of the door but he saw me right after that. I don't think it meant a thing to him until he saw me with you at the Bayview police station."

"Yeah," said Murdock, the old bitterness rising in his throat again. "I introduced you."

"He looked me up yesterday," Emerly said. "He said he wouldn't want to cause a lot of trouble for a friend of yours but he could use two hundred and fifty dollars to get to Florida."

"You could have paid him, couldn't you?"

"How could I?" Emerly said, his voice ragged. "That would have been only the beginning."

"That's where you went wrong," Murdock said. "Charlie was a little guy. He wouldn't deliberately harm anyone. If you had believed him you'd be clear right now. You never would have heard from him again."

"That's all right for you to say," Emerly said. "You never had murder hanging over your head. You're not the same guy when that happens; you can't even think the same way... I couldn't take a chance. That's the way it looked to me and that's how I had to play it. I still had the jewelry—I couldn't make up my mind what to do with it—and that's when I got the idea. I gave him a ring and told him to pawn it late that afternoon. I told him I'd make up the difference between what he got and the two fifty."

"All right," Murdock said, wanting to hear no more about Charlie Lane and trying to keep his voice under control. "What about Lucille Dunn?"

"She caught me in her headlights as she backed her car away from a bungalow."

"How'd you know who she was?" Darrow said, getting into the act for the first time.

"I got the license number... I made a lot of contacts doing those true-crime pieces," Emerly said to Murdock.

"It wasn't hard to find out the car belonged to Felix Dale and the address the bureau has was the Blue Heron. I looked him up Sunday before I came back here. I pretended I was a booker and said I might have something for the little blonde that worked there. He told me where she'd gone.

"I didn't know what to do about her," he added. "I probably wouldn't have done anything if it hadn't been for

Lane. But after that I got thinking and I'd gone too far then to have much conscience left. You don't know what it's like," he said desperately. "You get so you don't even think like a human being."

"I damn near caught you coming out of Charlie's," Murdock said, but Emerly did not seem to hear him. Instead he spoke of the one all-important thing in his mind.

"The book will be out a week from Monday," he said, half to himself. "I wanted to celebrate that day when it really became official. I wanted to see the reviews. Thirty years I knock myself out doing two-bit pieces to make a living and when I finally make it—even if it isn't all mine—"

"You can still read the reviews." Fenner's voice was flat and contemptuous. "All you got to do is put that gun down and pick up the phone."

"What?" Emerly's gray face puckered as he tried to follow Fenner's words.

"It'll take 'em months to try you and then you make a couple of appeals—that is, if the book earns some dough and you get a good lawyer. Hell, it'll be two years before the warden throws the switch. In this state they might even commute the sentence to life the way things have been going lately."

Emerly looked confused. He shook his head and his acceptance of the speech was literal.

"You don't understand," he said. "It's not going to be that way at all. It's like Kent said: I took the big gamble. All right. I lost, so I have to pay off. But not your way. Oh, no. I'm not going to be around when my publisher and the editors I know find out those stories they bought were not really mine. That's why I'm giving you a chance to walk out of here."

"Hunh?"

Fenner leaned slightly forward, the agate eyes speculative as he understood what the writer meant. He glanced at Murdock and Murdock shook his head. Darrow remained motionless in the wing chair but there was a watchful look on his face.

"I don't want to cause any more trouble," Emerly said.

"I've got nothing against you... Not even you," he said to Murdock. "I've run out my string but you're not taking me to the police. All I want you to do is get out of here and leave me alone."

Fenner gave him one long stare, shrugged, and stood up. "What the hell," he said. "Who am I to argue? I'm no cop. I'll have enough trouble talking my way out of this as it is."

Darrow pulled himself erect, the right hand still in his pocket. It was only Murdock who protested.

"No, by God!" he said.

"What do you mean, no?" Fenner growled. "Do you have to try to get that gun away from him?"

"This is my home." Murdock's bony face was tight and his tone was virulent. "I live here. I don't give a damn what he does but he's not going to do it here."

Emerly's bespectacled eyes were sick and incredulous.

"You mean I can go?"

"Now."

"But how do I know—" He glanced fearfully at Fenner and Darrow and they eyed him coldly and in silence. He tried again. "How do I know they won't try to—"

"Why should they?" Murdock argued. "They don't go around shooting people. They got trouble enough."

"Are you sure you know what you're doing, Murdock?"

Darrow asked.

"All I know," Murdock said grimly, "is that I've had enough. If that damn Bacon had got in touch with me or come around there wouldn't be any problem... Get moving, George," he said. "Once you're out of here you can call your own shots."

Emerly started backing toward the door but he still did not believe it. He kept the gun moving back and forth and when he opened the door and started to back through he said:

"Don't follow me. Don't try it."

The door slammed to punctuate the sentence and Fenner's gun came into sight. He moved quickly to the door and palmed the knob.

"Leave him alone," Murdock said.

"I just want to test him," Fenner said.

He opened the door but did not look out, which perhaps was just as well. Somewhere in the hall a gun slammed and a splinter flew a foot from Fenner's head.

Darrow meanwhile had stepped to the nearest window and threw it wide.

"Leslie!" he yelled. Then, a moment later: "There's a guy coming out with a gun. Watch him but don't take any chances."

Just what prompted Murdock to react as he did he could never explain. He had meant it when he said he was through, but something about Darrow's tactics and his warning prompted him to open the bottom drawer of his desk and pull out his Leica. He was at the other window a second or two later and as he opened it he saw there was still plenty of light in the sky. He set the shutter speed and aperture with a considered estimate of conditions and guessed at the distance.

What happened then was to some extent coincidental. Only later did he realize that the basic elements had already been arranged and the pattern set. Now, if he thought at all, it seemed that fate alone was responsible for the tragedy of errors that began to unfold on the sidewalk.

He was in time to see Leslie get out of Darrow's car and put the hood between him and the doorway. As he did so Emerly appeared, a foreshortened figure, the revolver still in his hand. He may not have realized how this would look, or perhaps he was still afraid that he might be followed, for he moved sideways, one eye on the entrance, the gun held in readiness.

At the same time, as if acting on some prearranged cue, two men stepped from opposite sides of a small black sedan parked fifty feet ahead. To one as experienced as Murdock that first glimpse was enough to tell him that this was a police car, that the two were detectives. A cynic had once said that cops looked like cops. It was that way with Murdock but he could not understand the reason for their presence until he remembered what Lieutenant Bacon had said: that he was having Darrow followed.

Even as the words came back to him the scene on the sidewalk began to unfold with a progression that was as swift as it was deadly.

A cruising taxi slowed to a stop in the middle of the street when the driver saw Emerly with the gun. His face was partly visible through the lowered window as he gaped at the two officers and awaited developments. Apparently alerted by Darrow's warning to Leslie, and having seen Emerly and the gun in the rear-view mirror, the detectives had reacted accordingly and now they moved. They unholstered their service revolvers as they closed in on Emerly, one near the curb and the cars parked there, the other close to the wall of the adjoining building, not knowing who he was or why he should have a gun but only that he must be disarmed.

Murdock heard someone say: "Drop it!"

He saw Emerly's tall form swing toward the voice, a threatening gesture because that movement pointed the gun.

Both men yelled: "Drop it!" again and now Emerly made his choice.

He may have intended to shoot and take his chances. He may have been too startled to obey; or it may simply have been his quick and knowing decision to die this way rather than do the job himself. Whatever the reason he must have understood the odds when he pulled the trigger.

Charlie Lane's .38 hammered and bucked in his hand. The two shots that followed almost simultaneously spun him about and he dropped the gun as the echoes died away. He began to sag as Murdock clicked the shutter and even then the impression came to him that Emerly had aimed high, that there had been no attempt to kill, that such an act had never entered his mind.

He fell over, collapsing joint by joint. He made one attempt to rise and lay still. Then, as the two detectives advanced, a car skidded to a stop opposite them. A voice yelled something and when the door opened and Murdock saw the hat, he knew that Lieutenant Bacon had finally arrived. . . .

When Murdock closed the window and started to turn away he saw that Jack Fenner had been watching the action over his shoulder. Now the detective shrugged expressively and blew out his breath.

"He was a lousy shot," he said, "but how come those town dicks were hanging around?"

"They'd been tailing Darrow."

"Well, what do you know?" said Fenner. "Funny how things sometimes work out just the way they should."

"You know where I keep the whisky," Murdock said. "Get a bottle. Bring some glasses."

He rewound his film and removed the baseplate of the camera. He took the spool out, slipped it into his pocket, and put the Leica back in the desk. By then Darrow had moved to his chair and this time when he sat down both hands were in sight.

Habit took Murdock to the telephone. He got his connection almost at once and spoke briefly in short clipped phrases. By the time he had finished Fenner came back with a bottle and four glasses. He poured whisky into two of them without asking and then glanced at Darrow.

"What about you, Carl?"

"Yeah," Darrow said.

Murdock was waiting on the divan, an empty glass in his hand, when Bacon came in and went into his act. He demanded an explanation, was given a brief outline of what happened, and replied profanely as he gave way to his exasperation.

"I had to get him to talk," Murdock said in rebuttal. "I had to make Carl talk. I didn't have too much evidence and—" He stopped, his gaze sullen and the stubbornness showing in his chin. "Where the hell were you?" he demanded. "Don't you keep in touch with your office? Doesn't the radio work in your car? If you had come around here a little earlier it wouldn't have happened this way."

The argument did nothing at all to soothe Bacon's ruffled f eelings and he turned suspiciously to Fenner. "What the hell are you doing here?"

"I'm working for Murdock, Lieutenant." Fenner made it sound respectful because he knew it would be a mistake to get fresh with Bacon under the circumstances. "Sort of an errand boy."

"I'll bet," Bacon said and glared at Darrow. "Okay, what's your excuse?"

Darrow adjusted his hat, glanced at Murdock, and took a chance. "He asked me to stop by."

Bacon made a muttered reply but he had not finished. He paced the room with stiff-legged strides, his hat had slipped off center, and his gray eyes were giving off sparks. He made threats he did not actually mean and spoke of charges that could be pressed, and Murdock made no protest until Bacon ran out of breath.

When he stood up the stubbornness still showed and his voice was flat and defiant. He understood the justification of Bacon's comments, but reaction was working on him now and his nerves were still jumpy and frayed at the ends.

"Okay," he said. "We'll do the rest of it your way. You don't have to front for me. Just remember that I've got a little something extra working for me."

"Yeah?" said Bacon. "What?"

"A newspaper. There'll probably be a picture of what happened outside but only the three of us know the real story. So you better make up your mind before we get down to headquarters. You can give out your own story. You can say the police closed in on Emerly and he was killed trying to shoot it out—which is about what happened. Or you can get tough and push me around and I'll write a story that gives the facts. Let's see how the department likes that kind of publicity."

He moved to the desk and poured out another swallow of whisky. To show there were no hard feelings, he pointed to the empty glass. "You want a touch before we go?"

Bacon wavered. He looked at Murdock to see if he meant what he said and right then he seemed to understand that the photographer was not fooling. He knew from past experience that when Murdock talked like that it was well to believe him and now, temporarily thwarted, he made an obvious effort to control his resentment. He glanced at the bottle, wet his Hps, and his good sense won out over his outraged feelings.

"You know damn well I never drink when I'm working." Murdock glanced at Fenner and the detective gave him the big wink. Behind Bacon's back he clasped his hands and held them up in a congratulatory gesture.

"All right," Murdock said, when he had gulped his drink. "You can have a rain check. If you're finished here, let's go."

It was nearly eleven o'clock before Kent Murdock came back to his apartment. There had been a lot of talk, mostly for the benefit of the district attorney. There had been some wrangling, and decisions to be made, and statements to be signed. Now, as he closed the door, he saw the glasses and the whisky bottle on the desk and carried them to the kitchen. When he had rinsed the glasses he made a fresh drink with ice and soda and took it back to the living room.

His eyes were tired and bloodshot, traces of beard were showing on his chin and the hinge of his jaw, and the strain of the past twenty-four hours had left his angular face slack and expressionless. He looked at the desk chair where George Emerly had made his decision. He looked at the divan and found it hard to believe that Lucille Dunn had sat there, not a month ago but only last night. He went over and eased down in the same spot and as his mind went back his fatigue became more bearable. He was still there some time later when the telephone rang.

He recognized the voice at once and the effect of it worked a small miracle on his flagging spirits. As his weariness momentarily vanished he recovered his sense of humor and when the girl said this was Lucille, he said:

"Lucille who?"

"How many Lucilles do you know?"

"The only one I know," he said, "is a blonde, seductive, and shapely number but her name is Dumpley."

Her laughter was a tonic and when she could she said:

"You must be feeling all right."

"I am now... Did you have a good flight down?"

"Perfect... I—did you get my note?"

"I got it."

"You're not angry?"

"No. I'm going to have to be more careful in the future but—"

"No, you won't. That's why I called. I wanted to be sure you weren't angry and to tell you it won't happen again. I'm in a hotel now but I'm going looking for an apartment tomorrow with another girl. If I write when I get an address will you answer it?"

"I might, if it's a real nice letter. I might even get down your way after the first of the year."

"That would be wonderful," she said. "I'll keep reminding you and you keep working on it."

Murdock said he would keep working. He thanked her for calling before he said good-bye, and when he hung up there was a fine warm glow inside him that had nothing to do with the drink. He found himself thinking of a Florida vacation as he undressed, but presently he understood that it was not the thought of this vacation that made him feel so good. The inner radiance came from the simple knowledge that she had liked him well enough to call him tonight and that glow was still with him a half hour later when he fell asleep.

THE END

THE FICTIONAL DETECTIVE
BY GREG FOWLKES

NOW AVAILABLE FROM
THE FICTIONAL PRESS

Read the first chapter!

THE FICTIONAL DETECTIVE
CHAPTER ONE

I was sitting in my office staring at the frosted glass of the door. It was a cold and rainy Friday morning in October and I had a hangover that made my head feel as faded and peeled as the paint on the walls. The half empty glass of Jack Daniel's wasn't helping my head any, but it was making it easier to ignore some of my other problems. Like how I was going to pay three months back rent on the eight by ten closet the landlord chose to call an office. Jobs had been pretty scarce lately. Even the divorce business had fallen off. No one seemed to care what their spouse was up to anymore. Not for the first time I wondered what the world was coming to.

A sharp rapping sound came that I thought at first was my brain shattering. A second later I realized that it was the tap of knuckles on the glass of the door. The lights were off in the office, and it couldn't have looked very promising from the outside, but the knuckles kept up the rapping. Looking through the "evitceteD ,EDALS KNARF", printed backwards on the frosted glass I could see the form of the rapper silhouetted by the sixty watt bulb in the hallway. It was a woman, and a good looker by the shadow.

The rapping stopped and the shadow moved away. I cursed myself for being too slow, but then she returned and rapped once more. The knuckles had a sort of desperate sound to them so I told her to come in, trying to keep my voice from sounding too harsh. The door opened hesitantly and she stepped through into the darkened office. She stood in the doorway groping for the light switch.

The bank of overhead fluorescents came on with a stutter and the light made me wince. I didn't mind so much when I got a good look at the dame. Her shadow hadn't done her justice at all. She was tall, looking taller on her spiked heels. Her eyes, a soft green gray would have almost been level with my own if I had been standing. Remembering my manners a moment later, I was. She smiled at my courtesy and her warm, red lips almost made my legs melt beneath me. Blonde hair curled under just at her shoulder line. I got a good look at it up close when I stepped forward to help her out of her coat; it looked natural. Everything about her looked natural though she was too good to believe.

I don't normally go overboard treating women with respect. These days it doesn't really pay, but this broad had class. Under her coat she was dressed in a black dress that clung to her like a sheath from her neck to her nylon clad calves, but despite the sensuous curves she looked like she was in mourning.

I held out a chair for her and then took one myself. Self-consciously I put the cap back on the bottle of whiskey and put it and the glass away in a drawer. "What can I do for you, Miss . . . ?" I couldn't see if she had a wedding ring on underneath her gloves, but I had the distinct impression that she wasn't married.

"Janet, Janet Nielsen," she said in a soft voice that reminded me of the taste of good bourbon — smooth and mellow but with a bite to it. "You are Mr. Frank Slade, are you not?"

"That's what it says on the door," I answered. She hadn't made a mistake. I had no illusions about my reputation and Miss Nielsen looked like she had the money and the class to get the best in town.

"I wish to employ your services if you are available, Mr. Slade. It's a matter of some importance to me and I am quite willing to pay you well if you can start immediately."

"I think I can shift my schedule, Miss Nielsen," I said, aware that I had no schedule or clients either. "What is it you want me to do? You didn't correct me when I said

'Miss', so I'm guessing you don't want me to check up on an errant husband. Or do you?"

"No, nothing like that," she said with a note of distaste. "A friend of mine died recently under mysterious circumstances. The police are saying that it was either an accident or suicide. I have reason to believe it was murder."

"Look, Miss Nielsen," I said, "I'd like to help you out, but if its murder, it's a business for the cops and I can't get involved. I could lose my license."

"But if the police say that it's not murder, then you are free to investigate. That's right, isn't it?" she said, assuredly. I wasn't used to getting that much logic out of a woman. "I will pay you two hundred dollars a day plus expenses. That will be adequate, I believe. I have a thousand dollars here as an advance against the first five days."

She opened her purse and pulled out ten crisp, new hundred dollar bills and laid them out on the blotter of my desk. I needed that money, but I was getting a little suspicious of the whole thing. It was too much like the opening of a detective novel; a beautiful woman, a hard boiled private investigator, a stack of brand new large denomination bills.

"Look, I'm still not sure I can do anything for you. Why don't I take a day's pay and check things out with the cops? If I think I can do anything for you, I'll come back and get the rest of the money. If not, we can call it even." I looked into those gray green eyes. She hesitated for a moment, and then nodded. I slid two bills from the pile, and then slid the rest back towards her. She didn't pick them up.

"Okay. Now why don't you tell me who this friend of yours was, and how he died?" I was watching her closely for her reaction as I asked.

"Do you know of Ezekial O. Handler?"

"The mystery writer?" I asked.

"Yes," she answered. For the first time she seemed to lose some of her composure. I wondered why. Handler was pretty well known as a writer. He had written a dozen or more books, a couple of which had made the best seller lists. I'd met him once or twice in the course of my work, but we definitely did not move in the same circles.

"Last night his car went off the road along West Shore Drive. They said it was traveling at a high rate of speed and crashed through the barrier. The car burned and Ezekial burned with it."

"That sounds like an ordinary traffic accident to me, Miss Nielsen," I said, trying not to sound callous.

"But it couldn't have been. He was a very good driver. He never took chances, either. Not stupid ones, at least. He wasn't the kind of man who felt that he had to prove anything, least of all to himself. No, if his car crashed there was a reason for it."

"If there was, I'm sure the police will find it," I said. I didn't like what I had to say next, she obviously had some sort of emotional tie to Handler, but in my business there are a lot of things you have to do that you don't like. "That is if it was an accident. It might have been a suicide. I didn't know Handler personally, but writers aren't always the most stable sort of people. It goes with the artistic temperament. Could he have had any reason for killing himself?"

"No, of course not," she said very defensively. "He had everything to live for. He was well off financially, he had a lot of good friends, he'd just finished his last book and it was one of his best. He stood to make a good deal of money from it, at least a million dollars. He was a happy man, Mr. Slade. I know that he was."

"Just what was your relationship to Handler, Miss Nielsen? Why are you so interested in proving that he was murdered?"

I thought she might clam up then or get huffy, but she said right out loud, "I was his mistress." Just like that, not like she was ashamed of it or anything. Maybe she wasn't. These days who could tell? "I loved him, Mr. Slade, and if he was murdered I want the murderer brought to justice."

I raised my eyebrows at that. Handler had pushed past fifty as far as I knew and he wasn't much of a looker, either. The pictures on his book jackets showed a nose that had been broken in fights a couple of times. When I'd seen him he'd proved to be a short man, though powerfully built. He had a reputation for getting into fights. He didn't seem the sort that would appeal to the woman across the desk from me, but like I always said, who can tell these days.

"I know what you're thinking, that he was thirty years older than me, but I never cared about that. He was always very good to me, kind and gentle. I admit to being a kept woman, Mr. Slade, but that doesn't mean that I didn't love him."

There was something strange about that phrase - kept woman - that seemed out of place. It was more like something from one of Handler's books than what a young, liberated woman should be saying. I didn't doubt that it was true, though. It would explain where Nielsen's money came from. Listening to her, I could believe that she had loved him, too. Either that or she was a mighty good actress.

"I'll take your word for it that he was wealthy and happy, but there are other reasons a man kills himself. What about his past? Could there be some secret there? Or his health? Hemingway killed himself because of cancer, after all." Handler wasn't quite in the same league, but I hoped the comparison might mollify her a little. The last couple of questions hadn't improved her opinion of me.

"I don't know too much about his past. He never talked much about it. He always seemed to live in the present. He's been a public figure for twenty-five years, though. I don't think he could have had many secrets.

He never seemed to care what people thought about him anyway, as long as they read his books."

"Maybe he cared about what you thought?" I said.

She smiled at that and I thought I was going to melt again. "No, I don't think so. He was fond of me, but the love was all one way. The only opinions that really matters to him were his own. He never seemed to mind the critics."

"What about his health, then? He was getting on in years."

"I can assure you; he kept in very good shape. He always ran four or five miles before he'd start writing in the morning. He was in good shape other ways, too," she said in a wistful tone that made me wish I'd been the late Mr. Handler. "He'd just been to a doctor a couple of weeks ago for an insurance examination. They must not have found any problems because he got the policy." I could believe her on that. Handler had been something of a physical fitness nut. I could remember the deep chest and the boxer's shoulders.

"Well, we'll rule out suicide for the moment," I said. "But he still might have had an accident. Some drunken fool might have run him off the road. It could have happened. If so, I'm afraid you'll just have to face it. But I'll check with the cops and go out and look at the scene of the crash myself. If I see anything suspicious I'll check up on it, Miss Nielsen."

"Thank you, I'm sure you will. Will that be all, now?"

"Yes, I think so. If I have any more questions I'll get in touch with you." She gave me her address and phone number, then rose to leave.

"Miss Nielsen?"

"Yes?"

"You forgot your eight hundred dollars," I said, though part of me was cursing myself for being a fool.

"Thank you, Mr. Slade," she said, picking up the bills and dropping them into her purse. I helped her on with her coat, smelling again the warm, sweet scent of her hair. Then she was gone.

THE FICTIONAL DETECTIVE IS NOW AVAILABLE
FROM THE FICTIONAL PRESS. FIND OUT MORE AT:

WWW.FICTIONALPRESS.COM

Resurrected Press Mysteries from the Dr. John Thorndyke Series

Dr. John Thorndyke - Lecturer on Medical Jurisprudence and Forensic Medicine. Before Bones, before CSI, before Quincy, M.E – there was Dr. John Thorndyke solving the most baffling cases of Edwardian London using the latest tools of medical science. Read about his cases in:

The Eye of Osiris
John Bellingham, noted Egyptologist has vanished not once but twice in the same day. Now Dr, Thorndyke must unravel the tangled claims on his estate, solve the riddle of the missing man and find the "Eye of Osiris".

The Mystery of 31 New Inn
When Dr. Jervis is whisked away in a coach with no windows to an unknown location to treat a man in a coma from undivulged causes it is Dr. Thorndyke who must come up with the solution.

The Red Thumb Mark
The first of Dr. Thorndyke's cases finds him trying to prove the innocence of a young man accused of being a diamond thief despite the fact that his finger print was found at the scene of the crime.

John Thorndyke's Cases
More cases of medical mysteries as told by his trusted assistant Jervis, M.D. Eight stories of crime and deduction in Edwardian London.

Visit www.resurrectedpress.com

About Resurrected Press

A division of Intrepid Ink, LLC, Resurrected Press is dedicated to bringing high quality, vintage books back into publication. See our entire catalogue and find out more at www.ResurrectedPress.com.

About Intrepid Ink, LLC

Intrepid Ink, LLC provides full publishing services to authors of fiction and non-fiction books, eBooks and websites. From editing to formatting, from publishing to marketing, Intrepid Ink gets your creative works into the hands of the people who want to read them. Find out more at www.IntrepidInk.com.